FINDING BICYCLES

I0603281

HEATHER PIPER

Finding Bicycles

DEDICATION AND ACKNOWLEDGEMENT

I would like to dedicate this book to my husband Rob who has listened to so many of my ideas with patience and given some very good advice about technology and how it may evolve in the future. I would also like to thank my friend Gavin for his editing and support. There are many others who come to mind and especially my favourite authors Raymond E Feist and Janny Wurts have inspired many of my ideas.

Finding Bicycles

CONTENTS

FINDING BICYCLES

PROLOGUE

As I sit beneath the full Moon in the garden that my father had created during his lifetime I absorb the cool energy She emits and I have time to think of other moments in my life when the Ritual Of The Full Moon was performed by the community of women in which I lived. Ten women drawn together by their beliefs and a need to draw energy from nature. There was a necessity, at that time, for much natural power in order to work the magic that had brought peace to the land after many years of turmoil. I won't dwell on that time, it will only bring memories that are best forgotten in time as we move on in peace throughout the world.

Oh it was a beautiful thing to be part of that work of ours. The intention was pure, the rituals performed with love and as there was no hierarchy among our community the way was always open for discussion on any topic you could think of. I do wonder now, in my later years, what happened to change our peaceful community. We had fifteen years of peace and love then….oh yes I remember how it began to fall

apart. I believe it was the day our new member arrived.

However, I shall start at the beginning of my adult life

and tell you the story.

CHAPTER 1 - BEGINNINGS

Many moons ago, when I was a girl of 15 years, my father – a good man - called me to him and announced that I was to be married in the next few months. This took me by surprise as I had no thoughts on the matter up till then. My life was good, I helped with the household chores, spent time with the animals in the house yard and had very little to worry about most of the time.   But there it was. My father was to marry me off to a young man about 140 kilometres away, so as was the way in our family, off I would go and marry. He was the son of a well to do land owner and although I didn't particularly like the idea, it was the way of our people and had been for a very long time. Father did tell me the story once of how it came about.

Apparently, in the many years past, there was a shortage of female children born. The scientists put it down to a reaction to chemical overload in the way food was produced and the chemicals used all over the planet as weed killers. Eventually there were almost double the males born to females so a plan was developed to prevent what was becoming dangerous practices of kidnapping young girls against their will to become wives. At the age of the girls consent, which was 15 years, a search would go out to find the right partner for her. Most of the time the boy would be of a similar age and social standing, although very rarely he would be older. This arrangement worked very well as the girl could refuse the man and some time was given for them to get to know each other before a marriage ceremony was held. It seems like a strange thing but for a few decades it seemed to settle the initial problem as the Elders of each community made sure it was not abused. Of course it was in some cases. I had read that centuries ago, this was also the practice and it continued for many years in some societies. Of course at the young age of 15 I hadn't read of the atrocities that were also a part of this system, such as in some religious communities where girls as young as 10 were married off to old men. However, I accepted this part of our family tradition as I had spoken to a few young girls who had married in this way who told me that in some cases the young man was very agreeable indeed. So when father made his announcement I took it in my stride. Oh how naive I was at the time.

At that age Father and our farm were my world. I was a healthy lass full of ideas and a need to explore my surroundings. We lived out in the country and there was always somewhere 'new' for me and had been since I was given free reign as a small girl. I had no real idea of what 'marriage' was and as my mother had died when I was very young I had little idea about anything else to do with this situation. Our housekeeper had done her best with me but as I say, I was very naive to think that this was how everyone still thought on the subject and of course they do not. Since then I have had a very long conversation with my father about how wrong it is to try and make people like each other enough to spend the rest of their days together and I do believe he might have changed his mind.

At least Father had found a young man for me and not some doting old widower (as had happened to a girl I knew). I resigned myself to the fact that this was to be, so went off to pack my possessions as I would leave in a few days' time escorted by my Aunt and Uncle to ensure my safe arrival. That was the plan. However, as it does, Fate was to intercede in a very interesting way.

Aunt and Uncle arrived a few days later in their cart and the very next day off we went. It was a sunny morning in Spring so the journey was going to be pleasant. I settled into the back of the cart with my possessions and a collection of packets and boxes that held my dowry. I was quite impressed by the amount of goods that came along with me, my father must have thought quite a lot of me, or so I deduced at the time. Aunt and Uncle were a nice couple and as they sat up the front of the cart chatting away to me we began to cross the kilometres. We covered quite a distance that day, trotting along at a reasonable pace, and eventually came to a travellers' hostel where we ate well and slept soundly, leaving early the next day.

The rocking of the cart must have contributed to me dozing off in my nest of boxes and packets for I awoke with a start, hearing my Aunt scream and my Uncle whispering frantically to me to hide under the pile of rugs I was travelling with and to keep perfectly still.

Being an obedient girl I did just that, and became very, very still.

A gruff voice called out and I felt the wagon lurch as my guardians climbed to the ground, my Aunt whimpering and my Uncle trying to calm her down. At this time I realised that the best thing I could do was stay put and stay very still. I was old enough and well informed enough to realise that a girl my age was not going to get off lightly if these men found me, and I was sure my uncle would try to protect me which could get him badly hurt or killed. So I stayed very, very still.

CHAPTER 2 – THE AMBUSH

That morning three men had dismounted and led their horses back into the forest. They tied them to trees and made their way back to the side of the road where their leader was still mounted watching the road in both directions. "You wait here for my signal," he snarled, "when you see me riding towards you hide in the bushes and be ready. I will cut into the forest and leave the horse with the others then join you. Be silent and you will be rewarded. I've been told there is a wagon on it's way with some bridal gifts on board. After we have the wagon you will take it to the spot where we camped last night and wait. If you touch any of the goods I will cut off your hand, or both hands. Don't forget that. Once I have made sure there is no evidence left behind I will meet you there." The three men knew the boss meant business so they nodded and grunted their assent. The leader then turned his horse and headed off down the road. "Well we might as well relax for a bit." said one of the men, "It could be a while before anything happens. I don't know about you but I'm going to have a sit down." He turned and found a clear spot and was soon joined by the others. However, it wasn't long before they heard the sound of a horse galloping at speed so finding their hiding places beside the road they waited. The dust told them that their leader was on his way and soon he came into sight, but not for long. He turned off the road and all was quiet until the wagon came into view. The men noticed an elderly couple in the driver's seat. Smiling at one another that this would be easy they waited.

"Stop right there," shouted one of the men, "get down and stand by the road." The elderly couple looked at each other and nodded. The men didn't notice the driver whispering something towards the back of the wagon before he climbed down. "Now stay there" they were told as one of the men climbed up and took the reins of the horse. Just then the leader of the gang came out of the forest. "Well done men" he said, "now you on the wagon go and one of you go with him. You there stay with me and we'll deal with these two." The wagon then drove off into the forest and the leader turned to the elderly couple. "We can't have you two running off and telling anyone who we are now can we. I'm too well known around here for you to be shooting your mouths off so I'm going to make sure that doesn't happen." Without another word he took a long knife from his belt and swiftly cut the throat of the old women. The old man just stood there with his mouth open in shock. He thought of his niece hiding under the covers in the back of the wagon and decided that silence was her best chance. "You coward" he said to the gang leader, "you kill old people who can't fight back. I do know who you are but you don't know who I am and there are important people who will be out looking for us. You will be caught and you will be dealt with. Meanwhile I will join my beautiful wife in the afterlife. Just know that you will be caught." These were his last words as the savage leader slashed his sword across the throat of the old man. However, wondering at those last words the leader signaled to the other man to help him and they dragged the bodies off into the forest. They returned to clean off any signs of the incident and then left on their horses. "We'll take the long way round," he called back "we don't want anyone following us to the campsite."

Rosalind remained as still as possible as the wagon bounced and lurched through the forest. She began to realise that she wasn't going to get out of this situation easily and her young mind began to imagine the trouble she would be in when they found her. Whether she would ever get to see her family again was in doubt and she believed that her aunt and uncle would not be allowed to live. Resigned to her fate she waited. Perhaps a moment would come when she could escape. Fear began to rise in her young mind. Although she knew what rape could do to a young woman she hadn't known anyone who had survived to tell the tale.

Her rough journey came to a halt after a fairly terrifying time being bounced about, feeling every stone and bump on the rough track. She held on tight to the rugs that were covering her body for fear of being found and when she heard the men's voices she held her breath for as long as she could.

"We'd better not touch the load till the boss turns up" one man said, "you know what he's like, he'll accuse us of taking more than our share. He should be here soon." "Right" said another voice, "we'll wait till morning then if he doesn't show up we'll take off into the hills and see what we have scored. Unhitch the horses and hobble them over on the grass. I'll get a fire going and we'll sort out some grub." Hearing this Rosalind sent a silent prayer of thanks to her Goddess that she hadn't been discovered and as the evening wore on she realised the men had stopped talking and decided they must have gone to sleep. Being so still for such a long time her legs and feet were cramped so she tentatively stretched her feet then when there was no outside reaction from the men she did the same with her legs. Waiting a short while she began the slow journey to the tail gate of the wagon, inch by inch, until she felt the space beneath her feet. Holding her breath she kept going, bending her legs towards the ground and hoping it was dark enough to cover her movements. Eventually, dragging her travel bag from the wagon she looked across to the campfire and saw the men sprawled on the ground under their blankets, fast asleep. However, she hadn't seen the other one standing guard amongst the trees. He turned suddenly sensing something was wrong and, taking his knife from the belt he wore he walked toward the wagon. Rosalind froze on the spot and as the man turned to look around the rest of the clearing she crept very slowly and quietly towards the trees. He hadn't seen her. Luck was on her side as a rabbit flashed across the clearing and into the forest on the other side. Visibly relaxing the guard put his knife away and went back to where he had been standing. He turned his back on the clearing and began to relieve himself against a tree. This was the moment for Rosalind and she silently vanished into the trees. For the moment she was safe but she knew she had to get as far away as possible before she could stop. The dark moonless night engulfed her as she now ran, hoping she would not make any sound that would wake the men.

CHAPTER 3 – ROSALIND REMEMBERS

In the dark one tree looks very like another, so I decided to keep the camp-fire at my back and just keep walking in the opposite direction. Running was tempting, however I didn't want to trip over some hidden root. I noticed a large bright star in the sky ahead of me so I aimed for that, thinking that was the best way to prevent me from going around in circles. Fear drove me at this stage, I could only think that if I went far enough away then I wouldn't be discovered. My body trembled and perspiration dribbled down my back as I took one silent step after the other. Luckily there were damp leaves on the ground to muffle my steps and as no-one was actually looking for me I felt that I could go on forever if I needed to. At 15 I had the bravado of one who had never actually been in any danger before and firmly believed that I would get out of this situation. So I kept walking, as fast and silent as I could with the thought that I would eventually be missed at the other end of my journey and someone would come looking for me sooner or later.

It seemed like many miles that I walked. Over meadows, through streams and woods until I was very weary. There was no way to know what time it was but I knew I had to stop. The moon had been high in the sky most of the night so damage to my person was kept to a minimum. However the woods that surrounded me felt safe, so finally I decided to rest. There was a little stream meandering its way through the forest, the moonlight glinting on the water so taking a drink of the cool water I found some soft mossy grass beside a fallen tree and curled up as close to the tree as I could, pulling my cape around me. I ate an apple from my meagre supply then, with the comforting thought that the robbers didn't know I had been there in the first place, I promptly fell into an exhausted sleep.

Something woke me suddenly – I wasn't sure if it was a sound, a touch or just a feeling. I sat up and looked around, taking a moment to understand where I was. At this stage I came to realise that my feet hurt and my legs ached from my hike through the night. My shoes were not for hiking, they were meant for normal everyday wear so the soles were badly scuffed and worn. I found that I had a small tear in my sleeve but apart from a few insect bites I had survived the night quite well.

The sun was beaming through the trees low down near the horizon so I realised that it must be early in the morning. I seemed to be alone, so whatever woke me was not to be seen or heard. Taking a drink from the stream I washed my face and took stock of my situation. With absolutely no idea of where I was I decided to cross the stream and head towards the rising sun. The path I took led me through a very peaceful woodland, with a dappled light touching the earth as the sun came through the canopy of trees. For some reason I felt safe, as I had during the night before. There seemed to be no danger for me so I began to relax and take in my surroundings. It was during this feeling of calm that I became aware of the distant sound of voices coming from somewhere ahead of me. I left the path I had been walking on and took to the bushes, making my way quietly towards the voices. I thought that perhaps I could get some help or direction, after all I had absolutely no idea of where I was or which direction I had come from. I didn't even know where we had been the day before when we were held up by the thieves.

As the voices grew louder I began to creep from bush to bush and tree to tree, being careful where I placed my feet so as not to give myself away. Then I stopped behind a thick bush because in a clearing ahead of me, bathed in sunlight were two young women. They were dressed in white robes, their feet bare and their long hair hanging loose down their backs. With hands held high and their faces turned up to the morning sun they were chanting words that I did not know. So rapt in their incantations were they that as I stepped from the shadows of the forest they seemed to be totally unaware of my presence, or so I thought. I watched in fascination and sat down on a fallen tree to wait for them to finish. The words they chanted seem to instil in me a sense of calm so I closed my eyes and listened.

Finding Bicycles

Soon I felt my mind expand until I could understand what they were chanting. Amazed and delighted I allowed this to continue until I felt a light touch on my arm. "Good morning Sister" said a gentle voice. I opened my eyes to see both of the women sitting beside me, I hadn't heard them coming. "You are most welcome to join us" the other said, "we are about to connect our energy with the Earth Mother to ask her blessing for our work today. Please, feel free to be with us. I am Marigold and this is Pennyroyal."

I think I must have looked quite shocked as they both smiled at each other then took my hands and drew me up to my feet. "I am so sorry that I interrupted your Ritual" I spluttered, not really knowing what I should say. "I have been walking since early this morning and I don't know where I am. When I heard your voices I thought you could help me." I then told them the story of my journey since leaving home two days ago and the frightening circumstances that separated me from my guardians. As I told the story it became clear to me for the first time that I could have been killed, or worse, so I sat back down and burst into tears. "Oh my dear" cried

Pennyroyal, "what a frightening experience for one so young. You are very brave to have escaped and made your way here. We knew someone was coming, the forest creatures let us know. They told us a Sister was on the path and that they had stayed with you last night as you slept, just in case harm came your way. Then they watched as you made your way here. Nothing happens in the forest that they don't see. So here you are and you are safe". With that she placed her arm around my shoulder and brought me back to my feet. "Now, what is your name child?" asked Marigold. "I am Rosalind" I replied, "but my father calls me Rosie." It was then that I realised, as did they, that we were all named for a flower or plant. Fate, once more, seemed to be guiding my way.

During their Earth ritual I stood quietly to one side. This was not my ritual, although I felt strangely comfortable in the presence of these women. Finally they finished their work and bade me go with them. We walked an easy path through the forest until we entered an enclosure through a wonderfully carved gateway. As I entered the enclosure I became aware of three other young women and two very ancient ladies. They turned as we entered and each gave a warm smile and nodded their heads in greeting. I felt as though I had come home. "We all live here together" Marigold explained, "our task is to work the energies of the Earth and other elements to bring peace and prosperity to the land and its people. We have been here since the Great Wars almost decimated mankind and that was followed by the terrible Ecocide brought about by mankind's greed. Our land was ruined by mining and chemicals until the Earth Mother began to fight back. You will have learned this ancient history no doubt and how mankind realised they had to return to simple ways or perish. The fuel that they used in their machinery was gone, chemicals and artificial food was killing off the people and the rubbish piles made life unbearable. It was no wonder that the final revolution saw a return to simplicity. It has been hundreds of years since the last outbreak of disease and the rising of the seas decimated most of the city populations and those who fled the cities found refuge in the countryside. Our group came from those people. Centuries ago our Order was asked to help the people to return to ancient practices of giving thanks to the Earth Mother. They called us Pagans then and as most people had lost faith in the organised religions who just kept saying their God would provide, but had no other answers, many folk decided to follow the older ways of looking after the Earth.

From those early beginnings we have joined with other women and men throughout the land to forge peace with our Mother Earth. The people have learned how to grow food without chemicals with the help of those who had been doing it for centuries and the farmers learned how to farm without taking all the natural growth from their farms, and without the machines and factories that polluted the atmosphere Nature has returned to a more moderate climate. We have heard ancient stories of the terrible storms and raging seas, of the forest fires and freezing blizzards that plagued the Earth for nearly 200 years. It took her a while but Mother Earth has seen that we are trying to live a simple life and She is now allowing that to take place.

Finding Bicycles

So my dear, you are most welcome to join us and learn the ways and rituals we use. You will share a hut with others, eat with us all and be free to come and go as you please. The only rules are those that make life comfortable living within a Community and those that affect Nature. What do you think? Will you join us?"

Well, I stood there trying to take all this in. My tutor had told me the stories of the time before, when machines and strange powers were the tools of men. He told me of massive buildings made of steel that reached for the sky and how they had crumbled to the ground or been engulfed by the seas when the ice melted. There were some books that showed these cities, my father had one locked away for safe keeping and he allowed my tutor to show this to me. The writing was strange, very straight and even. I was told it was "printed" by a machine. There were many tales of these times, however as the Earth began to recover a few hundred years ago, the people had come to realise that life was much easier living with respect for the Earth and each other. So there I was with a decision to make.

Finding Bicycles

"I would love to stay with you" I replied "though I think I should try to get word to my father that I am alright. He will be getting worried soon because I should have reached my destination by now. I am sure that word will get to him in a day or so that I have not arrived. Perhaps I can send a message somehow." "Yes" replied Marigold looking thoughtful, "we can do that. There is a village nearby and we can send a messenger to your father to let him know you are safe with us. I am sure he will know who we are. So if you would like to write down a few words for him I will see that it gets there." I was pleased with that and so my new life began.

After meeting the other women in the Community I was shown where I would live. The hut was round, with small windows under the wide eaves. The walls were made of straw bales covered in beautiful orange clay. It was cool inside, but cosy, with beautiful woven rugs on the floor that I discovered had been made there in the Community. There were four beds in the hut with a small stove in the centre, a table and four chairs with cups and a kettle and each bed had a box pushed under it for personal possessions. I was shown my bed and where I could put my things then taken to the bathing house that was set between the huts. Pennyroyal explained everything to me then left me back in my hut with a little pile of clothing.   There were three gowns for me to wear, one white for ritual work, one natural wool for everyday wear and one dark green for special occasions and going into the village. An apron to wear over the every day gown was made of plain flaxen linen. There were a pair of boots and sandals and three pairs of warm socks made from hand spun wool and to top it all off a large shady straw hat. After I changed into the every day robe I stashed my belongings into the box under my bed and went off to find my new companions. My life was to be a happy and peaceful one, but with many interesting turns.

I found everyone about to sit down to their morning meal and so I joined them. The food was very simple, crusty bread with a delicious jam that tasted of last Summers' berries. "We grow and make most of our food here" explained the elderly member of the group. Her name was Violet and I discovered later that she had

lived over 90 years, 70 of them there in the Community.
"You can spend today getting to know your way around
and tomorrow, if you wish, you can spend some time in
the garden. Although we don't eat meat we do have
chickens who have never been with a rooster, so we eat
their eggs. Our beautiful goats give us milk for our
cheese after their little ones no longer need the milk.
Our bread is made from flour we get from the village,
which we pay for with our excess produce. So you will
understand that our garden is very important and we all
like to spend time working there. So please, today just
wander about and ask questions if you wish." When the
others returned to their tasks I began to find my way
about. I was still quite tired after my ordeal but there in
the Community I felt safe.

After a few days a young man arrived at the
gate asking for Violet. He had a reply from my father so
I was summoned to hear. Violet bade me to sit by her.
"I'm afraid I have bad news my child," she said, putting
her arm around me, "your aunt and uncle were killed by
the thieves. A forester found their bodies. The Sheriff
has sent a search party for the killers, we will be kept

informed. Meanwhile, your father was told and he has said that the main thing is that you are unharmed. He said you may stay with us and gives his blessing. It seems as though your happiness is more important to him than anything else and he will speak to the family into which you were to be married. You are much loved by your father my child."

As I sat there tears began to flow from my eyes. My aunt and uncle were beautiful souls and they had died protecting me. "May I go please Mother?" I asked Violet, "I would like to be alone for a while if that is alright." "Yes of course child, I will see you later on." I left Violet and crossed the garden between the huts and felt suddenly very sad. I walked to the little Garden of Peace in the corner of the enclosure and wept for my aunt and uncle. It was some time later after gathering my thoughts that I heard a bell ringing that seemed to be calling in the Community. When I followed the sound I found it was time for the midday meal and it was then that I decided to make the best of my life here in this peaceful place.

CHAPTER 4 – MY EDUCATION

There was much to learn in those early days. I was taught herb lore so I may understand and respect the plants around me. The walks in the forest with one of the older women were fascinating as I was told to find certain plants then work out what they could be used for. I learned to be wary of the poisonous plants and how to use them properly. Many days passed quickly by as I became engrossed in my studies. At night I would lie on my back gazing up at the stars as Marigold explained how the sky changed as the year progressed and the "shooting stars" progress as they seemed to travel so far across the Universe was a fascination to me. I loved the full moon nights the best as we would hold a ritual to draw down the energy into our naked bodies. There was an ancient legend that men reached the moon once then years later a nation sent miners to the moon to steal her minerals. They had not been able to stay there very long because the fuel they used to transport the minerals back to Earth had eventually run out. Perhaps it was the Earth Mother's way of preventing her Sister the Moon from being ravished!

The Rituals I learned became an important part of my life. We would rise early to greet Father Sun and at sunset we would gather to bid him goodnight. We had many ways to thank the Mother which included the Solstices and Equinox celebrations. Ancient rituals handed down from the resurgence of Earth worship brought about by the Warming Days had grown into uncomplicated rituals that even small children could perform. From the farms and villages everyone took part in thanking the natural elements for the peaceful and healthy lives they lived.

One morning when I had been in the Community for two years I was called to Violet's hut. "Good morning Rose" the Elder said, "I believe we have found an excellent occupation for you. Would you like to go to the Village once or twice a week to teach the children how to read? Your reading is very good and you have some knowledge of the life outside our Community. At the moment there is no-one in the

Village who can read and write. What do you say?" "I would be delighted Mother" I replied happily, "books have always fascinated me since I was a small child. My tutor told me how important it is to read and I learned so much from our books." So it was settled, I became a teacher of children. I was given a book to take with me to teach the children. It was a simple little book written just for children. The pictures were painted in the colours of the Earth and the plants. The words were carefully written in an ink made from mixing different earth and ground stone and the 'paper' was made from flaxen linen and hemp. There were paper books, as this was what my father's books were made of, but the process of making paper had been forgotten over the centuries except for some that came from a far-away placc that had to be reached by many months travel including a journey over water. I had read about boats. The building of these vessels had not been forgotten in time, however, as we had no need of them in our part of the world the only way we knew of them was from books or from the tales of travellers.

Finding Bicycles

Walking to the village that first sunny morning filled me with pleasure. The path was clear and easy to walk as it had been used for many, many years. I passed a family working in the field who smiled and waved to me, calling me over. "We have found something that you might be interested in" said the man, "you may even know what it is because we haven't a clue". He pointed to the ground where they had been ploughing and there was an unusual metal object half buried in the ground. "We have never seen the like of it before, even though we are always unearthing bits and pieces when we dig up a new area." said the woman, "Have you any idea what it might be?" Well this was a new one to me too, so together we pulled and tugged until it came loose. Lying it on the ground we studied the object. "It looks like some kind of wheel" the man said, "but it is very heavy and I can't see that it would be much use on a cart with all those bumps on the outside. Even if we had four of them, I don't think I could use it like a normal wheel." We all studied the 'wheel' then turned it over and looked at the other side then poked around nearby to see if there were any more of them.

Finding Bicycles

"I'll tell you what" I said, "I will ask around to see if anyone else has found one and when I can I will send a drawing of it to my father to see if there is anything like it in his old books. Meanwhile, can you keep it somewhere safe until we know more?" They were quite excited that they had unearthed this amazing object and went off towards their barn dragging it along behind them. The 'wheel' was quite large, about a metre across and had notches all around its edge. It was about a hand width thick and was solid except for a hole in the centre. I sent a note off to my father when I got to the village and would usually hear back from him in a couple of weeks. The elders of the village had gathered many objects from ancient times. They kept them in a room behind the blacksmith's work shed that they called a Museum and once a month it was left open for people to come and look around. I had been inside and was fascinated by what was there. Some of the items I recognised from the books my father had and I had been allowed to put labels on them so others could know of the ancient past. There were people travelling the land who had studied these ancient times and knew what most of the items were. These Historians were due to come to our village soon so I would be able to talk to them. There were no restrictions on my activities in the Community, in fact I was encouraged to venture out and discover new things. As the youngest member of the Community at the time I had much freedom to explore and learn, so as a naturally curious person this gave me so much pleasure.

I arrived at the Village and, as was arranged, went to the Village Hall and rang the big bell that was there to call in the people. I was told to ring it only 4 times and that would bring the children, so I did just that. Within minutes children came running up to me from all directions. They were all smiling and laughing as they found places to sit around my feet. "Good morning children" I said, "are you all ready to learn to read?" They all nodded their heads. "Well, let us all go and sit under the big oak tree" I suggested, "the grass is soft there and the tree will shade us". Off we went and began our first lesson. When I produced the first of the books we would learn from they were very excited as none of them had ever seen a book, although they knew from their parents that such a thing existed. I had been told once that in ancient times people read their stories from mechanical "books" but these had died out when electricity was no longer available. There were many happy days spent with the children. I was able to teach them all over a time and believe that most of them would use that knowledge all of their lives.

During this period there were people in our village who believed that learning to read and write would eventuate in to the downfall of civilisation. I could understand this idea, we had centuries of peace and good health without the need of further knowledge. One day on my return I asked Violet what she thought about this and was quite surprised by her answer. "My dear, they have a good point," she said with a rueful smile, "there was an old saying *'knowledge is power'* and I agree that if knowledge is used in the wrong way it can lead to use such as keeping those without knowledge as servants or slaves. Yes it can be a bad thing, but it can also lead to everyone being equal if everyone is taught the same. Imagine," she continued "how life could be easier for, say, a farmer, if knowledge of plants and the soil could be available written down in a book that could be left in the local meeting hall for all to read. At the moment we have meetings to discuss such things as what to plant when the moon is in certain phases, what is the best way to store food and other knowledge. Now most farmers have this knowledge passed down from their mothers and fathers, but what of the people taking up farming for the first time, or perhaps moving away from the family to marry and settle elsewhere? These people could read a book specific to their area. Then there is another group, the healers. Although we in our Communities care for the health of our local people, what if the knowledge we have could be written down and given to other villages and communities so they could help the sick and injured?"

Violet smiled at me, understanding that I was perplexed that some people thought books were evil and unnecessary. "I can see that you are still worried" she continued, "so this is how I see what can be done. Why not invite the adults along to a meeting at the hall and explain what we are doing? This way they can see for themselves that reading can be a positive thing. Explain what I have said about good knowledge. I am sure you will win some of them over, but you will never win them all."

I left Violet to think over what she had said. I do remember my Tutor telling me of a time when women were forbidden to read in the Middle Countries. It was believed that if they could learn to read then they would no longer be obedient to their men. I had found this very disturbing as our culture had never differentiated between males and females. From birth the only difference was in what our bodies dictated. Women were taught the workings of the body as were the men, the only difference being around pregnancy and procreation. Boys were taught about birth and breastfeeding and were expected to support their partners. The household chores were everyone's responsibility, our minds were considered non-gender as were a lot of the garments the people wore. I had a male friend as a child who had no idea there was a difference physically because his mother had died when he was very little and he grew up to 5 years with only his father and brother, no women were in his household. It was only when we went swimming that he noticed we were built differently. His poor father had to explain it all to him when he went home. Oh that makes me smile when I think of it. The questions he must have had. His father hadn't thought of it before because males and females were all treated the same.

However, this did not help me to ponder the issue of reading. I decided to take Violet's advice and invite folks to come along to discuss the matter of reading. There would be an opportunity for questions and comments, so I would need to be prepared. I would put together some ideas and suggestions and would have food and drinks for the people to enjoy. This was to be very exciting for me. The next time I had the children about me I asked them to invite their families to come along on our Rest Day and to bring a picnic to share. The children were very excited and promised to try and bring as many adults as possible.

That Rest Day I rose early and after the morning meal I gathered up the few books and other writing samples I had gleaned from the Community and headed off to the Village. Many people had arrived and had arranged themselves in groups, sitting on blankets and tree stumps. They all looked expectantly at me as I made my way to the centre. Well, it went very well. I explained why I thought it was a good thing to be able to read and write and showed them the books I was teaching the children from. The discussion became very animated of course, there were a few there who were not convinced that we would benefit from this, but most people agreed that the children should keep learning.

I find it hard to believe, now many years later, that what began back then as a small class for children would lead to the reading that is being done in the land today. The generation of children grew up and made it a normal part of their lives. Now we have a small library and someone worked out ways to produce enough paper to make books of our own. Who knows how far it will take our people in the future.

CHAPTER 5 – HETIA

During this time, far away on the Plains of Parlat in a small village called Flessia the local Wise Woman, Hetia, was looking out the window of her cottage at the garden she so dearly loved. Many herbs grew in her garden as she would use them in the healing arts she had been practising all of her adult life. It was some years now since the Horde had been dispatched from the Plains with the combined arts of Hetia and the others of magic. They had been raiding the Plains for several years, killing, raping and pillaging as they rode. However, in the end they were no match for this powerful woman and others. The Horde had been sealed up in a cave where their fate was in the hands of an advanced nation who could transport them through the ether. They now lived in custody, never to return.

Finding Bicycles

Once the folk on the Plains realised that the evil ones were not going to return they felt it was safe enough to begin rebuilding their lives. A whole new generation of babies had been born over the last several years and farms were now restocked with animals from the sale yards over the mountains in the large town. Hetia was also rebuilding her life. Her relationship with Erik, the tall quiet man who lived in a hut at the bottom of her garden had developed into a deep friendship, a mutual understanding that it could never be anything more. Erik had been the first leader of the Horde, a particularly savage leader. However, his whole life had turned around as a result of spells and incantations from Hetia and others. When Hetia saved his life she brought him back to her home where he made the decision to put his past behind him and make amends. The folk of the Plains had accepted his plea and eventually he had gained their respect when he helped defend them against the Horde. They were simple folk and now he was one of them.

The weather was changing when Hetia stood observing her garden. It was time to get rid of the dead plants and put in some new fresh annuals. She loved this work and so she turned, grabbed her hat and gloves and headed out into the garden. "Time to do some work" she shouted towards the hut. "Come on Erik, grab your garden tools and join me." She felt a spring in her step as she made her way to the tool shed to collect her tools and soon she was joined by Erik. They stood quietly together looking over the garden until Hetia took a deep breath and turned to him. "Alright Erik, you get to pull out the big sunflowers and those plants over there and I'll start on the vegetables."

They didn't talk much during the day, they never did. This was the way of their relationship and it was well into the day before they stopped for some lunch. After a short while Hetia spoke as she cast her eyes over the work they had done. "Erik, I am going away for a while. I need to hunt out some supplies from the other side of the mountains and there are some healing plants that can't be found around here. There is a community of women healers who will have what I need and I may be gone for some time. I know it is safe to travel alone now and I will enjoy that freedom from responsibilities for a while. I will need you to look after the garden for me. You know what has to be done. When you pick the herbs you can dry them for me and store them in the jars, you have seen me do it. Any of the vegetables that are ready before my return you may eat them, sell them or ask one of the women to preserve them. It is your decision. I will need to put a protection 'cloak' around my cottage so that strangers do not see it, but you will be able to come and go as you please." She turned to Erik and placed her hands on his shoulders. "I shall miss you and I shall return safely." "Thank you for trusting me" replied Erik, "I will do my best to look after the garden while you are gone. And I will miss you too." He smiled then stood and made his way back to his hut. Hetia noticed that his shoulders had lifted a little and he seemed to walk a little prouder. She knew she could trust him now and although she cared for him very much she kept her vow of celibacy that she declared when finishing her training to be a Wise Woman. This was so very important to the work she did with the spirit world and she would never break that vow.

Finding Bicycles

The next morning Hetia set off. She had borrowed a reliable mare to carry her as it was a very long journey. Few folk were awake at that time of morning and those who were saw the horse and rider make their way slowly and quietly out onto the road towards the east. This was a chance to cast her mind back to the turmoil and danger that brought Erik into her life. They had been hard times for all the folk of the Plains and they had lost many friends and family during the reign of terror. This made her ponder on the fate of those evil ones, transported to another part of the world through a method she didn't even try to understand. The Captain, leader of the group who came briefly to the cave where the Horde were captured, had wanted to explain it to her many years before during their encounter within the safety of her "hiding cave", a place she had found the communicator that led to their first meeting. Hetia knew that there was so much out in the world that was left over from the Climate Catastrophe, so much that she felt her people were not able to comprehend and so she had declined the Captain's offer to take her there, to his world, his modern world, because she knew it would disrupt the peace they had found. It was dwelling on these thoughts that made her curious. Whatever happened to the Horde once they were taken away. Did she really need to know? "No you don't" she said out loud to herself, "your life is peaceful now, you have all you want and need and there is no point in upsetting the balance at this time." Realising that she was talking to herself Hetia smiled and urged the mare into a trot for a while. The horse must have realised it was time for a stretch of legs and took off with her head high and tail blowing out behind. They carried on like this for some time before Hetia slowed the mare and came to a halt. "Well horse, it's time for a rest. Now what did they say your name was? Oh yes. Alright Brightness it's time for a drink for you." She had spotted a little stream nearby and led the horse to it. Sitting down beside the stream Hetia felt around in her bag and found her drinking gourd and some nuts and settled down for a while. They were relaxing peacefully when she heard a rustling sound nearby. Placing her drink gourd on the ground she closed her eyes and felt out with her mind. "Aha" she said quietly, "you can come out you know, I won't hurt you." Within moments a small face appeared in the bushes nearby and a girl child of about 8 or 9 smiled at her. "Who are you?" asked Hetia. The child just smiled but did emerge from the bushes and came to sit beside her. "Are you from near here?" said Hetia but the child still did not speak. However, she pointed to Hetia's bag and then at her mouth. "Oh, so you are hungry are you?" said Hetia, "I can give you a little food but this has to last me a long way. I'll tell you what, you tell me where you are from and I'll tell you who I am." At that the child started making sounds that were almost words but not quite so Hetia began to use some signs with her hands and the child responded. After some time Hetia realised that this child had been living in the forest for some time, probably by herself. Through many hand signs and pictures drawn in the dirt it finally occurred to Hetia that the child had never learned to talk, she wasn't mute at all. "Well child, I think we had better find out who you are. Would you like to come for a ride on my horse with me?" Using signs to explain what she meant she picked up the child and put her in front of the saddle. She seemed

delighted at the prospect so Hetia climbed up behind

her and made her way. It would be half a day before

they reached a town so over that time they seemed

settled into a situation where Hetia would talk and point

and the child would nod or make a noise.

It was becoming dark by the time Hetia spotted

some lights ahead so with their newly found sign

language she asked the child if she had ever been there.

With a shake of the head she turned to Hetia who

noticed a frightened look on the child's face. "Don't

worry" said Hetia, "I will look after you, you have

nothing to be afraid of." They stopped at a little Inn

with a sign to say there were rooms for overnight and

Hetia lifted the child from the saddle. "Come on, and

you can hold my hand if you like." The child did just that

and they entered the Inn. "You are Hetia the Wise

Woman aren't you?" asked the innkeeper. "We do

remember you and the amazing things you and the

others did to get rid of the Horde. What can I do for

you?" "We would like a room for the night please."

answered Hetia. "My little friend here is very weary and

we are also very hungry so can we please have some food as well." "Of course you can" replied the innkeeper, "you can have the room upstairs at the front. It has 2 beds in it and has a nice window you can leave open. Dinner will be ready in a little while so why not put your things up there and come back down. Now I will not take anything from you for the room and food, you have done so much for the folk here that you can stay anyway. Now what about your little friend. She seems very quiet and shy and those clothes she is wearing are very ragged." "Well," said Hetia, "I found her about half a day's ride back towards Flessia and I have no idea who she is. I was hoping someone might know her. She doesn't talk so I can't get much information. Perhaps someone here knows her."

"That's interesting" said the innkeeper, "but first of all I have some clothes that my daughter grew out of years ago. Do you think she would like them?" "I am sure she would" replied Hetia, "and we will go upstairs and freshen up. Thank you very much. Come on little one, we have a nice warm bed for this night." She took the girl's hand and they climbed the stairs. She noticed the child's curiosity as they made their way and when they entered the room and Hetia put her things on one bed and told the child she could sleep on the other one she saw an amazing reaction. The child took the pillow from the bed and put it on the floor. "No little one, you can sleep on the bed." and she pointed to the bed itself. She was beginning to realise that this child had been in the forest for a very long time.

After a while they went back downstairs and the innkeeper handed her a bundle of clothes. "These should fit your little friend." he said, "I have asked about a bit and it looks like you might have stumbled upon the answer to an eight year mystery. During the raids of the Horde one of the local young women took a group of children into the forest for safety. They went deep into the bushes and trees but the Horde caught up with them. The young woman was, well eventually, killed but some of the children escaped. They were eventually found but because some were too young to tell the rescuers who they were they were taken to various homes to be cared for. One of the children who was about 5 years old at the time told her carer that there was a baby who couldn't walk and that they had to leave her behind when they ran away. They were not able to find her because the children were too young to find their way back. I don't know how she has survived this long but I think you have found that child." This was an amazing story and Hetia turned to look at the child. "Do you know how you have lived safely for so long?" she asked her. "You can't have survived on your own, you were too young. Can you tell me who has been looking after you?" The child looked puzzled but then it seemed to come to her. Grabbing a piece of paper and a pencil from the counter she began to draw pictures. The story came out in a flood. It appeared that she" had been living in a hut in the middle of the forest. The old man who lived there had found her and taken her back with him. He had fed her and kept her safe but when she was about 5 years old he had died and she had looked after herself ever since.

"I'll make some more enquiries around the village." said the innkeeper, "Meanwhile, here's your dinner so if you would like to sit over there in the corner I will bring you something to drink. Please, relax, we will get to the bottom of this." Hetia and the child sat where he suggested and ate the delicious meal that he put in front of them. They were settling in nicely when an old woman approached them. "Are you Hetia?" she enquired. "Yes" replied Hetia. "Then I think you might have my granddaughter." Tears were in the old lady's eyes as she looked over the wild looking child sitting there. "My daughter was killed by the Horde and I had given up any hope of ever seeing her daughter again. Her name is Alicia and she would be 9 years old in a few weeks." Hetia stood and led the old woman to a chair at their table. "Oh I am so sorry you lost your family but if this is Alicia then it is wonderful." Hetia also thought silently that even if it wasn't Alicia then it would do no harm for them to all believe it so. Turning to the child Hetia made up her mind. "I think we have found your family young lady" she explained to the child. "This is your grandmother. As I have a long journey ahead of me I think it would be best if you go with her and when I come back in a few months' time I can check up on you. How do you feel about that?" Knowing that the child probably had no idea what she was talking about Hetia turned to the old lady. "She doesn't speak because no one has ever taught her but look at these drawings." Hetia showed the pictures the child had drawn to the old lady and explained what she thought had happened. "So, would you be able to take her home with you and teach the child to speak? I am on a very long journey and it may not be very safe. I believe that this child is your granddaughter Alicia and I also believe she would be better off with her own people." "Oh I would be delighted to have her" replied the old lady. "The whole village lost so many people to the Horde and every life is precious." Turning to the child she said, "Alicia, and I know you must be her, will you come with me and live with me and your grandfather? We will find some nice clothes for you to wear and you can have a room all to yourself." Holding out her hand to the child she waited and it was only moments before the small hand was firmly inside the older one and turning to Hetia the lady said "You have made me so very happy and I thank you from the bottom of my heart. Please come and stay on your return journey, I can't thank you enough. Come on Alicia" and she turned leading the child out through the door where Alicia looked back over her shoulder and smiled at Hetia.

The next morning, very early, Hetia mounted her horse and headed back on her journey. She felt light of heart at being able to help the child and as it was a sunny day she found herself singing as they rode along. The rains had changed the land bringing out grass and wildflowers not seen for centuries. It seems the Earth had held the seeds dormant until the time was perfect. Everywhere was green with splashes of colour. Hetia felt blessed to witness such a sight and gave thanks to the Goddess for her patience. The land was being renewed. Her journey was peaceful as she allowed her horse to keep its' own pace. There was no hurry and it had been a long time since she had been alone with her own thoughts.

CHAPTER 6 – HEALING LORE

As my life was unfolding in the Community I began to become curious about the healing plants, so one day I accompanied Pennyroyal when she went into the field in search of herbs to dry for her healing stores. We set off before dawn as it is always best to gather some plants with the early morning dew still upon the leaves. This, explained Pennyroyal, gives special energy to the plants that can be enhanced by drying them indoors slowly. We gathered great baskets full that morning, then found a cool spot under a big Oak tree to rest and share the food we had brought. "Rosalind" said Pennyroyal, "do you have any knowledge of the medicine that was practised in the Ancient Times?" "No I haven't" I replied, "Well" she continued "from what I have read the healing was so very different to what we use today. The doctors and scientists – they were the people who searched for ways to make things work better, - had almost eliminated disease from our world. Little children were given medicine to prevent sickness and everyone took regular doses of mixtures so they would never get sick. It seemed that everyone would only die from accidents or when their bodies wore out in old age. However, what happened was that germs grew stronger and so did the medicines until it was found that the people were so full of these preventative medicines that they began having other problems. They couldn't digest their food properly, they had trouble sleeping and they began to develop growths in their bodies called Cancers. The medicines were stopping the bodies from fighting off these other problems. All except for the folk living naturally. These were people who had been practising the ways of Nature. They took their medicines from the plants as we do today, their food was produced naturally as we do with animal manure and composting, and most importantly, they cared for the environment by building smaller homes from the trees they grew for that purpose and the stones and mud they found on the ground. They made their energy somehow from the sun and being outdoors a lot these people were the ones who survived the upheavals of the Climate Calamity when the cities were abandoned and those people who didn't know how to live from the land began to starve. They just didn't know how to feed themselves. The people who practised the natural ways began to teach others how to grow food, build shelters and live without their machines. They also taught people to honour and thank the Earth for her bounty and they showed them their healing plants. All this is the knowledge we still have today hundreds of years later."

I took all this in and thought long on it. I had already learned of other knowledge of the Ancients, which seemed to end in disaster and it certainly made me feel lucky not to have been alive then.
We made our way back to the Community carrying the baskets of plants and took them into Pennyroyal's herb store hut. There were many bunches of herbs hanging from the roof in different stages of drying and along the walls were rows of jars full of ground up and dried plants. "Can you lay the plants out on the bench please Rosie?" Pennyroyal asked, "and try to keep each type separate from the others. The dandelion roots will need to be dried so you can take them outside and put them

on the table out there in the sun. Once they are dried we will grind them up."

I gathered up the roots and after removing the leaves took them outside to dry in the sun. When I returned Pennyroyal had gathered the dandelion leaves into two bundles, tying them with string. "Now please take these to the kitchen as we will use them fresh." I must have looked blank so she smiled and explained, "The leaves are really nice in a salad, and they are very good for you to keep your liver healthy. You know what your liver does don't you Rosie?" "Yes, I think so" I replied, "doesn't it make sure your blood is strong?" "Yes that's right" she replied, "and one of our older women has a bad heart so it's good for her too. But it does just taste nice." She smiled with that so I left her and walked to the kitchen carrying a large basket with some fresh leaves and flowers for our lunch.

As I walked, the sun warming my skin, I allowed my mind to wander. The thoughts were of the past, what it must have been like living without knowledge of what the Earth Mother could provide. So much is taken for granted now. A young child could find food if it was left alone. We grow up with the knowledge of seasons and moon times. We are taught nursery rhymes and stories as little children in order that it becomes second nature to us. I thought of life in huge cities where the sunlight would hardly shine between tall buildings and my imagination could not fathom what that must have been like. I had read in Father's books of machines that people rode in and smiled at the delight of riding in a cart pulled by strong horses. (Except of course of my frightening experience with the murderous thieves). Yes, it is much better that we now live with an abundance of fresh food and clean fresh air. I was content in my life.

Leaving my basket in the kitchen I returned to learn more from Pennyroyal. On my return I found her grinding some dried leaves in her mortar and pestle, a large stone dish with a beautifully smooth stone that fitted perfectly in her hand. I thought that one day I would have such a beautiful tool and be able to produce the herbs for healing and cooking. 'Yes' I thought 'I would be happy to spend my days doing this'.

I spent many days learning from Pennyroyal until one morning I was asked to attend Lavender. I found her in deep conversation with a woman I had not seen before. "Ah Rosie" she said with a big smile, "I would like you to meet Hetia. She has come down from the Plains of Parlat to seek some of our herbs and to trade with the villagers. You may be interested in her knowledge. So today will you please spend some time together, look after her needs and see that she has somewhere to sleep while she is staying with us." I had never seen anyone like Hetia before. Although there were tales of people who lived many days ride up towards the mountains and over on the Plains beyond. She was quite tall, in middle age with long reddish brown hair down to her waist. She had a streak of white hair going back from her left temple. Her hair was plaited with feathers and stones and there were strange symbols tattoos on her face and arms. The clothes she wore were of rough earth coloured fabric and animal skin trimmed with coloured beads and her feet were encased in soft leather boots. As she walked with me I felt her power and I found myself feeling taller. She obviously was aware of my curiosity and seemed to draw me into her Aura. She was fascinating.

"So Rosie" began Hetia, "we are to be companions for a few days. Would you like to begin by showing me around your Community?" "Of course" I replied "I shall start with where you will sleep so you can leave your bag and cloak there." I led her to my hut where there was a spare bed. "There you are, and there's a box under the bed for your things" I pointed out. "Thank you Rosie, I will leave my cloak but my bag is always with me." Hetia pointed out. As she spoke these words I felt a strong energy as if a protection was being drawn around her. Strange, she hadn't spoken any words or drawn symbols as I had seen others do.

We walked around the Community so Hetia could find her way and ended up in Pennyroyal's herb store hut. The two women greeted each other as the old friends they seemed to be so I left them alone and went off to attend to my normal chores vowing to find out more about Hetia and the people of the Plains.

Those days were very interesting. I spent many hours with Hetia and learnt so much. On the day of her departure Lavender came to me after the Greeting of the Sun ritual. "I have decided we can free you of your chores for a while Rosie. Would you like to travel with Hetia to her village on the Plains to learn more of her ways and her people? I believe all is safe there these days as the bandits that used to plague them have been seen to by the Mages." I must have looked a bit stunned as Lavender laid a hand on my shoulder. "It's alright" she said reassuringly, "I thought you must have knowledge of this. I am sure Hetia will tell you all about it on the way. Now, would you like to go?" "Oh yes" I gushed "that would be amazing. How long will I be away?" "Well that depends" replied Lavender, "Hetia often comes back in Spring so you can come back with her then. That is six moons away. What do you think?" "Six moons, yes that sounds like quite an adventure. I will pack my bag and be ready to travel very soon." So excited was I that I nearly missed breakfast until one of the older women called me to the kitchen. "Are you going to eat before you leave us Rosie?" she said with a smile, "It's a long way on an empty stomach." I filled up my very empty stomach and as I was leaving the kitchen

I was handed a large bag of bread and fruit for the journey. Out in the yard there were two ponies ready for travel, one with two large sacks thrown across it's back. These were full of the herbs and young plants Hetia had come to us for, and as the journey would take us a couple of weeks we had more food supplies in the saddle bags. I had changed into the warm winter trousers we wore when the weather was cold and they were very comfortable for riding in. I liked wearing trousers as it made me feel able to do anything that a gown would restrict. A few of the younger women wore them all the time apart from ritual as they found them liberating. So, with my bag of food on one side and my travel bag on the other we set off for the Plains of Parlat. I was very excited as I waved goodbye, this was my next great adventure.

On the way Hetia explained to me the problems they had experienced several years ago with the band of ruffians and bandits. They had created havoc over the Plains, terrorising the people, burning the houses and stealing anything they could carry off. This had gone on for quite a few years but eventually the people began to fight back. Following great meetings of all the peoples of their land it was decided that the only way to fight these men was to use methods that did not endanger their peace loving folk. They had found a Bard who came from the forests and taught them how to use the energies of the Earth to stop the onslaught of terror. By using the force of Nature herself they learned how to create landslides, whirlwinds and other seemingly natural disasters to finally rid themselves of the bandits. Hetia explained that her people had retained the magical side of our Earth based beliefs and each village had a Shaman or Wise Woman who acted as both a healer and protector. I was fascinated by this and enjoyed our journey as she told me the stories of how they had finally lured the bandits into a cave where they were sealed off by a landslide and, although her people had no idea of the final fate of the bandits, Hetia had arranged for them to be transported to a far distant land that was kept peaceful by an army. This transportation had been achieved by technology that had developed with knowledge kept from the ancient times. In order to maintain a feeling of safety this knowledge was never passed on and remained Hetia's secret until the day she passed over to the next life. She only hinted at the method to me on that journey, however we did spend time together many years later on one of her visits to our Community. We had often spent time together, she would teach me about the use of natural magic that would always be a secret between us.

So it was that we spent our time on the road, chatting for many hours and using the nights where she taught me meditations to gain strength from the Earth herself. Peace had reigned throughout the Plains for several years at that time and although Hetia had played a large part in the war against the bandits she was now settled into her life as the village healer.

CHAPTER 7 – THE PLAINS OF PARLAT

For six moons I stayed out on the Plains with Hetia in the village of Flessia. I believe this was the beginning of an amazing phase of my life. The people of the plains had long since become self sufficient for food and everyday living as they had been isolated from others for over 200 years. I was told of the early settlers who had been searching for ideal farmland and found the edge of a vast plain with a mountain range all around it. Through their chosen isolation they had developed their own ways, their clothing, food and language was so new to me, although I found I could understand most of what they were saying. I am sure I spent the first week with eyes wide open and questions on everything I came across. Hetia was very kind to me and tried to teach me many new things.

Hetia's home was a wonderful stone cottage. When we arrived I was not really aware of it until Hetia intoned a mantra whilst walking in a large circle. I was fascinated to see that what I thought was a pile of rocks suddenly appeared as a cottage. Seeing my surprise Hetia explained. "When I leave home for a while I ask the Spirits of the Stone and Earth to place a protection around the building. As I explained to you on the journey here there was a time when we had thieves and murderers in these parts, so I had to protect what I could. It is very simple really, the house is always there but to all but me it will appear as a pile of rocks until I ask the Spirits to reveal it. The art of 'cloaking' was one of the early things that I learned when I was training to be a Shaman." She smiled at my surprised expression and led me indoors. It was cool inside and a little dark but when my eyes became used to it I looked around. Hanging from the rafters were bunches of herbs and other plants and lining the walls were shelves laden with jars. I noticed that there were glass jars, remnants of times past as the only glass being made now had to come from another country over the water. These jars were very old and had turned yellow with time. The contents were varied, but I did notice 2 or 3 with what looked like baby animals that were too little to have been born properly. Seeing my curiosity Hetia explained. "I have learned that certain problems seem to happen if a creature is born too early, including human babies, and I am studying some of them that died to see if I can find out why. One of my tasks is to help a mother bring her new baby into this world and if it comes too early it usually dies. So by studying these little animals in the jars I might be able to find out how I can save them". This was so very interesting to me so I was determined to follow up in the future. Meanwhile Hetia showed me where to put my belongings and where I would sleep, then she took me around the Village. I noticed a small hut behind her house and pointed it out. "That belongs to a dear friend of mine" she explained and left it at that so I didn't pry.

A few days after my arrival Hetia called me after breaking fast. "I am going to gather some wild plants today on the Plains so if you would like to get your hat and a water skin you can come with me." she said. "I am particularly looking for a cactus, you may call it Aloe, and as I need a good deal of it we will take the little cart."

We set off with me pulling the cart, and headed off onto the dry land. As we left the village behind I began to experience an amazing feeling of peace. The air was still and our footsteps seemed to be the only sounds that could be heard. After an hour or so Hetia stopped and pointed ahead of us where a large cactus like plant grew. "There's one" she said, "we will take only what we need and leave the plant to heal itself." We went on and when we reached the plant Hetia took a large knife from her belt and placed it on the ground near the base of the plant. Placing both hands gently on the plant she began an invocation. I didn't understand the language but became aware of the meaning. I had also been taught how to ask for forgiveness from a plant and the Goddess before cutting into any plant then to give thanks for the gift. Feeling confident I went to the opposite side and performed my own rite. Hetia smiled and nodded her approval then with her knife she sliced off two large leaves of Aloe and placed them gently in the cart. Turning back she gave thanks to the plant and poured a small amount of water on the ground near its roots as a gift. I was pleased to see this small ritual as we didn't include the gift of water at home. Water was plentiful in the forests, although this was not always the case. I had read in Father's books that in ancient times, when the climate of the Earth was at a serious level of danger the rains had changed their natural pattern as Mother Earth desperately tried to save herself. In countries where the seasons were defined as wet and dry the wet season had become a lot drier than before and the plants began to die off. As the trees that had survived the logging began to die off in the forest massive wild fires wiped out what was left. Rain forests began to die through the heat and lack of water and the deserts broadened. On the other side of the world the opposite occurred as the rains became consistent, the hurricanes and massive storms did so much damage that the people stopped living outdoors. This led to gardens and forests being ignored and farms only growing crops with short seasons. Most vegetables and fruit were grown in massive grow tunnels covered in 'plastic'. We had only read about plastic in books as it had disappeared hundreds of years ago. There were some places that were recycling what was left of the plastic but it was unreliable and degraded very quickly.

Eventually the people of the world could only change their ways or perish, so more people began to listen to those wise to Nature and in time any who would not change began to suffer illness and financial ruin, this brought on the collapse of the cities. Those who had embraced the changes survived to become our ancestors, giving up all the ways that had damaged the Mother Earth. I had read of these changes. They grew their food without chemicals (these were man made products that poisoned the Earth and the people who ate the food grown with their use.) The people began to re-use everything they could until things finally rotted into the soil to feed the worms. The big shopping markets where the people had to walk long distances or ride horses to get there were replaced by the village markets we have today. Houses were then built to keep out the heat in summer and keep the cold out in winter. Some folk even built underground. It took nearly 100 years to change but they did it and now the waters run clear and strong following normal rains, the crops grow in the fields with animal manure and the trees now cover the coastal lands. We still have storms but not the big damaging winds and flooding rains that were experienced all those centuries ago. Out on the Plains the scrubby plants had returned and the rains came when they were supposed to, filling creeks and ponds. I only hope that we as a people never make the mistakes again that once beat the Earth Mother into fighting back. When I had read of these times in my father's library of books I made a quiet promise to myself that I would travel one day and see how different people had adapted to their new life.

In the six moons I stayed with Hetia I learned many things. She showed me the plants that were native to the Plains, the animals that they relied on for food and leather, I learned to make mud bricks to build with from a young woman who was extending her house and I learned how to catch rabbits with the children. Eating meat was essential to the survival of these people but they did understand when I declined. Their Spiritual beliefs were very interesting so I took the time to study this. Coming from the land of their ancestors gave them a connection, and although their people had gone through the stages of following organised monotheistic religions they had reverted to Nature for their spirituality when they returned to the land after the great Climate Catastrophe.

Looking back on my time on the Plains I understand how it is possible to rely solely on what is available close by. The people did not have any neighbouring villages so they ate what they could grow or catch and anything they could trade at an annual meeting of the widespread villages. It made me appreciate the lifestyle we had, being able to trade regularly with others, to meet each other for learning, pleasure and our Spiritual gatherings. We could buy timber or other needs to build houses, we traded with a village where cloth was woven and were able to enjoy food from faraway places when the traders came through our area. So much was taken for granted. People like Hetia who travelled far were able to take goods back to their villages on the Plains, but that was only two or three times a year. However, I was struck by how happy and content they seem to be. The children may not have learned to read but they knew more about animals and plants than any children I had taught to read.

CHAPTER 8 - BACK HOME

My return from the Plains was heralded by a wonderful event. It was a celebration of a successful harvest and the whole village and our Community were to be involved. There would be a feast on the village green with games and music and there was so much to do – food to make and gather, flowers to pick and make into garlands for our hair and an opportunity to wear our white gowns. I was no longer the youngest in the Community as we had gained a young girl who wished to devote her life to the Earth Mother. Her name had been changed to Daisy and she was just 12 years old.

Daisy and I were asked to gather the flowers for our hair garlands so one sunny morning with baskets on our arms we headed off into the meadows that bordered the road into the Village. At this time of year there was an abundance of flowers growing wild so I decided to use the exercise to teach Daisy how colours are used in our healing work. I explained to her the very ancient practice of Chakra Balancing to maintain good health. "We have many energy centres in our body called Chakras. That is from an ancient language called Hindi. But for now I shall explain the major ones that are from the top of your head right down to where your tail would be if you had one, (Daisy giggled at this thought). We know there are seven of these that we try to work with and you also have them in your hands and feet. There are others also but we won't worry about them at this time. These Chakras are like little spinning whirlpools, like the one in the forest that is very deep at the bottom of the waterfall. When your body isn't well, or your mind is a bit upset, these little 'whirlpools' slow down. They get kind of stuck. This can have all sorts of effects on your body and your mind. Many centuries ago the healers re-discovered how to use colours, crystals and plant oils to clean up these Chakras and allow them to spin again. This in turn would help the body heal up so the person or animal could then find ways to stay healthy. Do you understand so far Daisy?" I asked. "Yes" she replied, "I think I do. So if I was feeling a bit ill or sad one of our healers could use one of those things you mention to help me get better." "Yes that's right" I answered "so today we can talk about the colours of different flowers and how they can be used. Now let's see what is growing around here. Oh look, there is a wild rose over there with red flowers, we shall start there."

We went to where the wild rose was rambling against an old fence. There had been a house on this spot once long ago and the fence with the red rose growing wild were one of the few things remaining. I took my cutters from the basket and cut two of the flowers. "We won't be able to use these in our hair with those thorns Daisy, but we can use them for decoration." I explained. As we walked along I explained how we use the colours of the flowers for healing and I noticed after a while that Daisy was looking a bit confused. "I remember how hard it was for me to learn so much" I sympathised, "tell you what, let's just do one colour each time we come out and you can think about how you can use that healing energy in between our walks". Daisy looked a bit happier at that so we sat under a shady tree and ate the food we had brought along. On the way home we picked a basket full of flowers for the festival and spent the rest of the afternoon with the others making decorations. There was much chatter and laughter amongst the women as we all looked forward to the celebrations.

The next morning we all rose early to take care of the last minute cooking and decorating. Together we gathered up our festival decorations and food, piling it into our market cart that was already decorated with ribbons and flowers, then in our best white gowns we headed off to the village with our little pony wearing her flowers through her mane pulling the cart.

What a day it was. There was music and dancing, tables really groaning with piles of food and many games for both the children and the adults to play throughout the day. The favourite game for the families was the three legged races. I was asked to look after a game of 'knock em downs' where the task was to knock over a stack of wooden blocks with a ball. It was a lot of fun and not so easy because I made the adults stand a fair way back to throw the ball. During the afternoon many of the elderly folk and the little ones fell asleep under the shady trees then at the end of the day, tired and happy, we loaded our empty plates and all our decorations back into the cart and headed home. Oh, I did love those festivals and I still do although these days I am not so able to join in the physical activities that I did then.

On our return that day there was a man sitting outside the gate to the Community. He seemed to have been there for some time as he had nodded off to sleep leaning back against the wall and his horse was unsaddled, grazing nearby. Our chatter and the rattle of the cart woke him up suddenly and he seemed quite embarrassed at being caught asleep. "I am sorry for the intrusion ladies" he said, "but I have a message for one of your members. Is there a Rosalind with you?" He looked from one of us to the other, obviously not able to recognise me. "Yes" I answered, "I am Rosalind. What is the message please?" "It's your father miss" he replied, "he wants you to come home as soon as you can. He has something very important to discuss with you and he needs you at the house so he can show you something first." "Well," I said, "I assume this can wait until the morning. We have guest quarters where you can stay and food and drink will be provided for you and your horse. Please follow us in and bring the horse, we have stables."

As we trundled the cart through the gate I was very curious. It was clear that the man didn't know what my father wanted so I would have to wait. I went to see Violet after helping to put everything away and she beckoned me to sit by her in front of the fire. "Do you need someone to go with you in the morning my child?" she asked, "You will be travelling a few days with this man who you seem not to know. Perhaps it would be wise to have a companion along." "No thank you, I shall be alright" I assured her, "I remember that I have seen him before in our Village, he works with our law-giver so I am sure I will be quite safe. We will stay in hostels at night and it will only be a few days. We will leave after breaking fast in the morning. Thank you for caring." With that I kissed her goodnight and went off to my bed. I didn't sleep much that night wondering what was so important for my father to send for me. I had been at the Community for a few years since I had seen him and I worried that he might be ill. Still, I would have to wait and see what fate had in store once more.

CHAPTER 9 - ADVENTURE

Three days later, tired and ready for my old bed we arrived at the gates of my father's house. I was quite excited to see my father and the house again. There were many happy memories for me there. As we neared the house my father stepped out, his arms wide to embrace me and a glow of happiness in his eyes. "My beautiful Rosalind" he cried, "I am so happy you were able to come. Let me look at you, oh you are so grown up and beautiful." We embraced then walked arm in arm into the house, just enjoying being together once again. However, my curiosity was too strong to wait so as soon as we crossed the threshold I turned to him. "Alright Father, what is so important that you needed me here in such a hurry?" "Come into the living room" he replied, ushering me before him. "Sit down and relax. Would you like some refreshment? It has been a long journey for you." "No, thank you Father," I said, now getting concerned that he had become ill and didn't know how to tell me. "Alright sweetheart, I am quite keen to talk to you. I have been asked to take a long journey to meet with some people who want to trade with us. These people live quite differently to us and I thought you might like to come along with me. The journey will take several weeks and includes some sea travel. They are people who use boats all the time and live along the sea shore. Some refer to them as The People of The Sea. There are mountains behind their town so farming is difficult. Somehow they learned that we grow very good grains, wheat and oats and as they can't grow any of these and they do have things we don't, such as dried and smoked fish and excellent basket ware, they suggested we see if a trade agreement can be achieved. They also make excellent carpets, rugs and fabric made from the wool of the sheep and goats they farm. I had a visitor some weeks ago with a letter from their company of traders so they also have a knowledge of our language. One of the reasons I want you to come, apart from the pleasure of your company, was that you can help me to write up any Trade Agreement that is made. Besides, I thought you might like a new adventure!" He said these last words with a twinkle in his eye, the same twinkle I remember as a child when he used to encourage me to mischief much to the chagrin of my nanny.

After a moment to allow Fathers story to sink in I smiled and replied, "Well, this is very exciting. I would definitely love to go with you. I have brought my things with me as I didn't know how long I would be here and we don't need many possessions at the Community. I will need to send word back to Violet so she will not be concerned about my long absence. So, when do we leave?" Father was amused at my enthusiasm, "As soon as we can arrange transport," he replied "which should be only a few days. I will send the same man back with your message to Violet if you would like to write something down. We will give him a day to recover though. However he is quite used to travelling. Now, what about clothes? You probably will need some as I don't think the few things you left behind years ago will fit you now. I see you have taken on the robes of a Priestess, so please let me know if you need more appropriate travelling things." "Thank you Father" I said with a smile, "but I am quite comfortable as I am. Personally, I find that people, men especially, leave me in peace when I am out and about dressed like this. However, perhaps I can find some warm trousers to wear underneath, especially for travelling and cooler weather, and a pair of warm boots would be helpful. Otherwise I am ready to go! Now what was this that you wanted to show me?" "Ah yes" he replied, "I have an old map of the world in an Atlas." he explained as he went to his desk and picked up a large book that I remember spending time with as a child. "I can show you where we are going." He opened the book to a page and explained to me where we were on the map and a town that was by the sea, then ran his finger across the sea and pointed to another place. "As you can see it is a reasonable distance and will take a couple of weeks at sea. As neither of us has ever been that far before it will be quite exciting, don't you think? We will leave our horse and carriage at this town where the boats come in, I have been told they will look after them very well. I have already booked our passage on the ship because I knew you wouldn't be able to resist the idea of an adventure. I have been worried though that you might be concerned for our safety. I know it has been some years since you were attacked on the road and we have never had a chance to talk about your Aunt and Uncle who were murdered. They never caught those men but I would imagine they are long gone from this part of the country by now. Do you have any fears for our safety?" I smiled at Father and threw my arms around him, giving him a big squeeze. "Oh Father" I gushed, "we will have an amazing time together and I have long since come to terms with that problem. So long as I am with you I will always feel safe." However, I have to admit that it was in the back of my mind.

Next morning Father gave me some money to spend and I went into the local village to buy my warm pants and boots. The pants were made of wool woven to be very warm and fitted cosily into the top of the boots I bought. I added a couple of pairs of warm socks just for good measure. Although I would normally stay away from animal skins I am quite content to wear those made from animals that have been killed humanely for meat.   I felt a bit strange wandering among the people I had last seen as a girl, and I did get some strange looks in my Priestess robes. Father had spoken to a few people about my staying in the Community so there were many who greeted me as an old friend. With the money Father had given me I stopped at the fruit stand to take home fresh produce for the next few days. Father's gardener grew many things to eat but there were some delicious strawberries that had come from miles away and I knew we would enjoy them with some fresh cream when the cow was milked that afternoon.

With my purchases stowed away in the big bag that was now my constant companion (it held all manner of things) I set off for home. I had found a lovely soft neck scarf in the same shop as my woolly pants so I bought this for my father. Walking along the pathway I began to recall other times that I had ventured this way when a young boy came running towards me. "Please miss," he panted, "your father sent me for you. He has organised transport and you are leaving after the midday meal today." "Oh, thank you, Tomas isn't it? I will hurry along. Why don't you walk with me and tell me all the interesting things that have been happening on the farm while I have been away."

We walked together with Thomas chatting away about the farm. He was a happy and friendly lad about 13 summers old. His father looked after all the other workers and his mother was the cook for our household. However, since I had left home my father had moved them into the main house and ate his meals with them. My old Tutor, who was getting quite ancient now, had begun to teach Thomas and his sister Sarah how to read and write. This was quite something for children of farming families who had to work on the farm from the age of 8. So Thomas had a lot to tell me and the journey seemed so much shorter.

The house was buzzing when we arrived home, food was being packed for our journey and I had to hurry and get my things together. The scarf was happily received by Father who wore it proudly- even though the day was quite warm. So after the midday meal we climbed aboard the carriage that was to take us across country for the next four days. Waving goodbye to Thomas and his family, I was once more in the hands of the Fates.

Finding Bicycles

Crossing the country in a comfortable carriage for four days with Father was quite pleasant, if I ignored the bumps in the road. We stayed each night in warm, clean accommodation and enjoyed some good company along the way. This was the first time I had been able to spend time in Father's company since becoming an adult and I know this pleased him also. We discussed many things, including the upcoming sea journey, which excited both of us. Oh what an adventure we were embarking upon.

On the fifth day we came over a rise in the road and there ahead of us was the harbour. I had never seen the sea before and Father hadn't seen it since he was a boy. To my eyes it was amazing, so much water. I had seen a large lake but this was so different. As we moved towards the small town that looked after the harbour I was intrigued by the way some of the houses were joined together in rows. They had a footpath made of hard white "stone" that my father said was called concrete, and their front doors opened onto these paths. There were many horses and carts, some full of goods, and others only large enough for 2 people just like our carriage. Then I saw a wondrous thing. It had two wheels with a frame in between and the rider sat on the seat and pushed with his feet to make the wheels go around. Father said it was a bicycle and that once there were many of them. However, the factories that used to make them had closed a few centuries ago so the ones here had been kept going by using other ones for parts. There had been so many originally that enough had survived. I did think it would be wonderful to ride a bicycle and I did get an opportunity to do so much later in my travels. But that's another story.

As we neared the water we pulled up at an Inn where Father explained we would be able to stay until the morning when our boat would arrive to take us on the sea. The horse and carriage would stay at the Inn so we could collect them on our return. Having been in a carriage for four days it was nice to walk about. Father and I left our baggage at the Inn and went for a walk through the town. The people were much like those in the village near where I lived, although we had no paved streets or houses joined together as they were here. Before long many boats began to arrive and Father explained that they were fishing boats. They had been out to sea all day and as they tied up many people began to arrive with baskets over their arms and proceeded to purchase the fresh fish directly from the boats. It was quite industrious for a while, then as the people left with their purchases the sea birds arrived waiting for the leftovers. One was very cheeky as he swooped in and stole a fairly large fish for himself. The fisherman yelled and waved his arms at the bird but to no avail as the bird and his prize rose beyond his reach. There was much laughter and teasing amongst the fishermen and even the victim of the pilfering had to laugh in the end. As we lived so far from the sea I had never seen such a sight before, there were fish to be caught in the river not far from Father's home but I had never even eaten a fish.

We sauntered back to the Inn for our last sleep on dry land for a while and as the last few days had been a continuous journey with overnight stays in different places, I did sleep soundly that night. The next morning we were taken to the ship with our baggage and there I stopped to take a good look at what would be our transport for the next seven days. All wide eyes and (probably) open mouthed I climbed up the gangway.

CHAPTER 10 – AT SEA

The journey on the sea was fascinating. My father was concerned that I would be unwell aboard, however the Captain of the ship said I had very good "sea legs" and that I was a natural sailor. Once we were out to sea the Captain was happy to spend time chatting with us. We were the only passengers on this journey. The Captain explained that centuries ago large ships the size of small towns sailed the sea driven by mighty engines. These engines ran on fuel that was eventually phased out as oil from the ground dried up across the world. They had made artificial fuel for a long time and oil was being made from vegetation that was enough for lubricating machinery, however eventually people returned to using sails once again for sea travel and some even had small windmills that drove engines set below decks. I would learn how much the wind was being used for power as we travelled about. Ships had been propelled by wind for thousands of years before the engines were invented and still worked very well. The captain told us how the old steel boats had eventually rusted and been sunk at sea and the newer boats once again were made of wood. I was happy about that because I had no way of imagining a steel boat run by an engine because I had only read about this in books.

Our cabins were quite small but very comfortable, however as the weather was nice we spent most of the time up on deck and only went to our cabins to sleep and change clothes. The boat was powered by mighty sails and I spent many hours watching the sailors working the ropes and pulleys that kept the boat moving along at an amazing speed. We passed a few small hamlets as we sailed near the coast, but they were too far away to see them properly.

After fourteen days at sea we arrived at our first destination. I was leaning on the railing as we neared the dock, watching the men ashore as they stood ready to catch the thick, heavy ropes used to tie the boat safely to the dock. On board two of the sailors stood beside the huge coils of rope, one at each end of the boat. At a signal they both threw what appeared to be a ball attached to a light rope towards the men ashore who then caught the balls and began to pull. All of a sudden the heavier ropes began to descend to the dock and were securely tied up. The job was done very quickly then the gangway was put in place for us to walk ashore. Father called me to collect my belongings as we had to be ashore as quickly as we could so the Captain could catch the outgoing tide. I decided that I could happily travel by ship and would endeavour to do so as much as possible. The Captain explained to us that he would be back in three days to pick us up so we went ashore for the first time, for me, in a different country. We said goodbye to the Captain and admittedly I looked forward to what the Fates had in store as we headed into the town. Before very far we were approached by a rather distinguished looking man who held out his hand to Father and gave me a beaming smile. This was the man who had come to see Father about the trade agreements.

It is interesting that although this was a different country to ours, so many things were familiar. The people spoke a different language but a few had travelled and knew our tongue and a language I was told was known as the 'common tongue', a mixture of our language and others. I was able to learn this language during our travels and was to use it most of the time we were over the sea. The houses were mostly built of stone and were quite small, their roofs were thatched and the people themselves seemed to be almost primitive in their dress and habits. I mentioned this to Father and he agreed. I discovered from a guide who had been provided for our stay that these folk had been living the same way since the Great Climate Catastrophe. The sea had taken away their town and much of the farming land. They were a simple people even then. So being isolated from most of the world they put their energy into starting over. Stone was plentiful so it became their main building material with windows and doors salvaged from the ruins of the old town. Sheep and goats grazed the hills and fish was plentiful, and so they were content.

On the second day we were taken to a large building where we discovered their "industry". The windows of this building were very large to allow lots of light in, so when we entered there was sunlight streaming through those windows. Placed around the room were large weaving looms. Most had work on them and the "click-clacking" of these looms as they were used was very loud. Our guide suggested that we look around so off we went. There were beautiful patterns emerging on carpets and lengths of cloth. I stopped to watch an old lady who was making a carpet. The colours were dark reds and browns and the patterns were familiar to me. I had read one of Father's books that showed rugs from a very ancient country called Persia that were reproduced by the people of Old Turkey, so I asked the old lady, with the help of our guide, where she had learned of the pattern. She smiled and explained that it was passed down by her mother and grandmother and had been passed down for hundreds of years beforehand. She said that her ancestors came from a village in Turkey that practised the old ways and was very pleased that I knew of the pattern.

As she worked the old lady related the story of how in ancient times the girls of Persia and later Old Turkey, began weaving a carpet as soon as they were big enough to handle a loom. The pattern and colour would show where the girl came from. When she was to be married she would finish the carpet and it went with her on her wedding day. She assured me the story was genuine and as her village kept the old traditions she had done this very thing herself.

Old Turkey had eventually become one of the most modern countries in the world, however it was so vast that there were still outlying villages where many things didn't change. The Climate Catastrophe had little effect of those people so the old traditions were still practised in many towns and villages. This had a big impact on me as I had read many stories of city folk who had no idea how to survive when the seas rose and flooded many cities on the coast. They fled inland where they had to find new lives. Eventually they would learn new skills, growing food, tending livestock and building their own small homes. However, these ancient crafts like carpet weaving were the domain of cultures such as we were visiting. Some of the patterns were kept secret and only passed down in families such as this old lady's. It was such an honour that she shared her story with me.

The following morning Father was to meet with the Elders of the town to work out a trade deal so I was left on my own to explore. It was with much anticipation that I began with a trip to the market in the town centre. There were many wonderful stalls with all sorts of fruit and vegetables I had never seen before and live animals like chickens and pigs snorting and clucking in their cages as people poked and prodded to see how lively they were. There was bright coloured clothing hanging from awnings and beaded jewellery dripping from stands onto the tables. Boxes of rings and bracelets invited customers to try them on and little places had been made with hangings in front to enable the trying on of clothes. There were so many things I had never seen before that I would not have been surprised if my eyes were bulging as I tried to take it all in. Our guide had given me some local money to spend so I began by purchasing some rather interesting looking fruit they called Figs, and as I bit into one the juice dribbled down my chin as it burst open. I admit that since then I have tried very hard to find this wonderful fruit as I do believe it was the most amazing thing I had tasted to that date. We were able to take some dried figs home with us and even eating them sparingly they didn't last long although I kept one for the seeds and although it took several years I did eventually have my own tree. Oh yes, I became quite fond of Figs. Wandering about I arrived at one of the stalls selling the bright clothing and trinkets and I decided my Father would look very interesting in one of the brightly coloured scarves they sold, so I chose one and went on my way with my purchase tucked into the bag I always carried over my shoulder. I could have spent many hours in that market, however it was a lovely sunny day so it wasn't long before I sought the shelter of a little place selling cool drinks. Under the shade of a large tree I sat and watched the people passing by going about their daily business. There was a group of children playing a ball game on the grassy area that seemed to have been made for the purpose of the game. The ball was kicked along the ground and as it came towards me there was a little girl in hot pursuit giving it a kick now and then to make it move faster. It came directly towards me and I stopped it with my feet. The child stopped dead in front of me and gave me a big smile then began to chat away to me in her own language, of course I didn't understand a word she said. However, I picked up the ball and threw it back in the direction she had come and with a squeal of delight she chased off after it. Just then an old man sat down beside me and began to talk. "I'm sorry" I explained, "I am a visitor and I don't know your language." He smiled and changed to my language, "Ah, you are one of the visitors that have come to trade. I was a sailor when I was young and came to your land quite a lot. I learned your language from a young and beautiful woman. She was so pretty and although we spent many days together she would not leave her country to come here with me so sadly I had to leave her behind. I have wandered many years and often wondered what happened to her but it was not meant to be for us to be together." He sighed and closed his eyes for a moment then opening his eyes and with a face that was beaming he said, "But that was long ago and I have been very happy in my long life and eventually met a wonderful woman who became my wife. That was my granddaughter who spoke to you, she was asking if you wanted to come and play with her but it seems she was happy just for you to throw the ball for her." We sat and talked for a while then he invited me to bring Father along that evening for a meal with his family. I felt very pleased that I had made friends with a local resident, I do believe this is the best way to get to know more about people and places.

Later that day I met up with Father and we walked back to the weaving centre. After long discussions about the difficulties of sending goods backwards and forwards across the sea an agreement had been made with the Town Elders to send a shipment of carpets and fabrics to Father and he would send back a shipment of dry goods that had been harvested by our farmers. We grew wheat, barley and various beans that were dried and stored for future use so a value had been decided that enabled us to go and choose the goods that would be traded. Father asked me to assist him in choosing the best selection as he wanted a woman's opinion. His reasoning was that women seemed to know more about carpets and fabrics than men – his idea not mine – and although this was a very old fashioned idea I went along with it, after all I did enjoy touching and looking at all those wonderful fabrics. When we were looking over the carpets I noticed that some were not finished so suggested that we order them for future delivery. Father thought that a wonderful idea and began to look closer at the colours that were being woven in. One carpet really caught his eye. "Look at this one Rosie" he exclaimed, "the colours would suit our living room at home wouldn't it?" I smiled at him and suggested that it would be quite alright for him to spoil himself with something for home. As Father was usually the one to be careful about over indulgence it was nice to see that he could relax this ideal and add something he really enjoyed to his home. So of course we ordered this one carpet but Father insisted that he pay for it with local money that he had procured that morning from the local money exchange. This worked quite well for travellers like ourselves. Father had brought along some rather nice ancient jewellery that he intended to exchange for local currency so he felt very happy that he could now purchase something for himself.

As we were making our way towards the section that stored the bolts of cloth I spied a rug with a beautiful pattern. The centre of the rug had a picture of a fat little man with a bald head sitting cross legged. Around this figure were symbols that were like writing but the like of which I had never seen before. I couldn't help but feel peaceful as I looked over the rug and wondered at how this could be. The colours were quite vibrant reds, gold and green, so determined to find out more about this beautiful work I called over our interpreter. "Can you please find out more about this rug for me?" I asked, "It seems to be writing of some sort." He asked me to wait whilst he went for some help and I found that I couldn't walk away from this piece. Soon the interpreter brought an old woman back with him. She was quite excited that I was drawn to the rug and began to explain, chattering quickly to the interpreter. He explained, "The rug came to the village with a trader some years ago. It is very old although it has only ever been hung on a wall not laid on the floor.

Finding Bicycles

There was a race of people who lived near the mountains called the Himalayas before the ice melted during the warming. They did not worship gods but followed ancient teachings of a man called Buddha. This is the man on the rug. The words are in a very ancient tongue called Sanskrit and, although no-one here can read the words, it is believed they are his words. He taught that all things can be solved peacefully and it was his teachings that led to the great Peace Pact that was signed by all the world's nations over 800 years ago. People had been fighting over religion, land, money and domination for thousands of years with no peaceful outcomes. One day a simple woman who followed Buddha's teachings came to the United Nations with a plan for peace that was based on respect of all spiritual beliefs. It took 20 years of her life to achieve this goal, but achieve it she did. It is believed that the words on this rug are the words of the Pact and although we cannot read it we understand the meaning. The reason it is amongst the rugs to be traded is that we have made a copy for our people and now it is time to pass it on."

Finding Bicycles

The story was quite amazing and of course I really wanted to take the rug home and pass on the story. I thanked the old lady and explained through our interpreter that I would speak to my father about it. Intrigued by all of this I found Father who had walked on to a back room to choose bolts of silk and gave him my old 'sweet daughter' smile that I had learned as a child usually worked. "Father" I said in my 'persuasive' voice, "I am very excited by a rug and I would like you to come and look at it with me please." He smiled as I took him by the arm and practically dragged him through to the rug. As I began to relate the story his face brightened as if with recognition. "I have read of this Rosie" he explained, "in fact it is in a history book that I have at home. It was the beginning of the end of organised religion. The people had become disillusioned for many years over the tactics of many religions and began to go back to asking for blessings from the natural world, which of course is how your Community and others like it developed. Once the hierarchies and organisations were disbanded peace was inevitable. People worshipped as they may with no discrimination. This woman you speak of travelled the lands of the Earth speaking to the people, in simple words that explained how peace could be achieved by following very simple rules of humanity towards others. She finally achieved her goal before passing from this world. It is a beautiful story and, although the telling of it is long lost, we still abide by those simple words. Yes we will take the rug and we will take it with us rather than leave it with the other shipment. It is beautiful isn't it? I will see what we have with us that can be traded." I was so happy that I had been given the opportunity to pass on this wonderful story and felt that I had managed to do my little bit towards future peace.

After we had finished choosing fabrics for clothing and curtains Father went off to do the trading and I went back to see the rug once more. I would try to understand the words and perhaps try to find out more about the teachings of this Buddha and the woman who had achieved the Great Peace. We spent the next day finalising our Trade Agreement and making sure everything was in place then set off once more in our boat heading for home with our beautiful rug

stowed in our luggage.

CHAPTER 11 - SHIPWRECKED

The weather was not being kind to us as we

spent our second night at sea. The wind became very

strong, blowing into the sails with a fury that was quite

amazing. I had always enjoyed watching storms and had a fascination with the amount of power that nature could use to assert her dominance over humankind. As I held on to the railings with all my might the dark ominous clouds gathered overhead, spreading in all directions to the horizon. Soon the seas became very rough and the rain began to fall in torrents. Father came quickly to my side and insisted that I move inside our cabin, and I admit that by then even I was beginning to be a bit worried. It was one thing watching a storm on land from inside a building that was built solid and another altogether to be on a boat bouncing around in a storm at sea. Father knew my passion for nature in her wildest so with gentle pushing he explained that the sailors would have enough to do without worrying about me on deck. I decided he was right and it would be a very good idea to take his advice and go below. Once there we changed our drenched clothing for something warm and dry then I spent a moment asking the Spirits of the Sea and Wind for a bit of calming, so balanced on my bunk I began to chant quietly a chant I had heard used during a very violent storm a few years before. The words didn't have any actual meaning, they were more like sounds, but they felt full of energy. So with my eyes closed I was not aware that Father had entered the room until I realised his voice was joined with mine. His deep resonating chant gave strength and power to mine so that I began to feel the energy resonating through the cabin. I have no idea how long we kept this going until suddenly there was a loud 'crunch' and a grating sound, with shouting voices raised above the wind. Everything went still and we seemed to no longer be at sea. The storm must have passed as there was no wind and thunder but suddenly a loud banging on our cabin door confirmed the feeling I had deep inside that something was definitely wrong. "Come out quickly" the voice shouted, "we have been dumped ashore by a huge wave and we must get off the ship as quickly as possible."

Father pushed open the cabin door and grabbed my hand firmly in his. The boat was beginning to lean over and it was hard to keep upright as we made our way up to the deck. Looking around we saw that we were now at a very steep angle and the side of the boat was resting on the sand. We had to scramble along the deck to reach the gangway and all the ropes and things that were lying on the deck had slithered down to the lowest railing. We certainly were high and dry but thankfully the rain had stopped and the deck had begun to dry out. There was much shouting from the captain as he attempted to make the boat safe. He ordered the anchor to be thrown high up onto the beach and sent men to tie the heavy ropes used on the docks to the trees above the tide line. He was obviously worried that a large wave could come and wash the boat back into the water and it wasn't in a seaworthy state. Turning towards us the captain called out, "Ah, you are both safe" he said "I am glad you aren't hurt. We lost our way in the storm then just as I was getting worried that we would end up on rocks a huge wave just picked us up and dumped us unceremoniously, but in one piece, onto this beach. I am making sure we don't get washed back out until we check that there is no serious damage. It was quite amazing really, almost like the sea itself was bringing us safely to shore. Anyway, we are safe so if you would please climb down the rope ladder to the sand and wait up on the beach a bit we will get the ship safe and bring your things down for you. I believe there were lights up there on the hill a way so there may be a village where we can get some help. I have sent a couple of the lads to see."

Well, what excitement. Here we were on a beach somewhere, I had no idea where, but it appeared that we were safe, or so the Captain seemed to think. He had proved to be a capable Captain so I saw no reason to panic. Not being one who shied away from a bit of adventure I had decided to make the most of this new situation. Father was looking like he was wanting to help the sailors secure the ship but didn't want to leave me alone. "It's alright Father" I assured him, "you go and help and I will be fine here. He looked a bit relieved and off he went. I looked around me and, of course, couldn't help myself as there seemed to be some exploring to be done. I would keep the ship in sight at all times as I remembered my close encounter when I first left home, and would stay within calling distance. This of course also kept Father happier as he could see that I was safe. There wasn't much to look at and the sky was still a bit dark but as the horizon began to lighten up I went off to explore. Before long I found a pathway leading away from the beach. This was the direction the sailors had taken when they went for help and although I didn't wander along it I found a small hut near the path. Being a curious soul at heart I tried the door and found it open. It seemed that it was a storage shed for fishermen as there were ropes and baskets stacked neatly along the wall and fishing nets hanging from the ceiling. There were two folding chairs leaning against the wall and some utensils that suggested someone prepared and ate food in the hut. As the light became brighter through the door with the rising sun I could see quite well and began rummaging around. I was sure no one would mind if I borrowed a couple of things so I picked up one of the chairs and an old but clean blanket and took them out on to the beach. Wrapping myself up against the cool of the morning I sat and watched Father and the men at work making the ship steady and reasonably upright. Once more I was given over to the hands of Fate.

Finding Bicycles

As the chilly early morning gave way to the rising sun to thaw out my cold feet and fingers the sailors returned from their trip inland. They had found a small village and had brought back a few men and women with ropes and tools. These appeared to be farmers and fishermen so I assumed the hut I had rummaged through belonged to some of them. Over the arms of two of the women were large baskets that, I discovered with delight, were laden with bread and jars of honey and jam. This was definitely accepted by all and sundry who had been working for a couple of hours trying to save the ship. I rose from my chair to greet the group in order to explain my 'borrowing' but was acknowledged with a smile and a signal that it was alright and to stay seated. I decided it was a good idea to stay out of the way, leaving the work to those who knew what they were doing. However, I did make myself available to help hand out the food. By now the sailors on the beach had also started a roaring fire so we gathered around it and boiled water for tea.

After this delicious breakfast I retreated to my spot up the beach to watch the proceedings. The women worked as hard as the men and watching them I

began to realise that I had lived a fairly easy life.

However this must not have bothered me too much

because it was halfway through the morning when, with

a start, I realised that I had nodded off to sleep and

some time had passed. Father was coming towards me

across the beach with two large cups and a bundle

under his arm. "I thought you might be getting hungry

again" he said with a smile, "you were fast asleep when

I came before so I left you alone. This is food left over

from breakfast so here you are". He sat down on the

sand beside my chair and setting down the two cups of

hot steaming tea he opened the bundle to share. Inside

was a large bun filled with deliciously smelling fried

eggs. I must have looked very surprised as he explained.

"Amongst the food the villagers brought were freshly

laid eggs in case we needed more food later on, so the

ship's cook has been busy concocting this delicious

feast." By the time Father finished his story I had already

devoured my share of this feast. I did remember this

when I finally returned home and introduced it to my

companions in the Community.

Finding Bicycles

As we sat quietly on the beach I turned to Father, "Have you had a chance to speak to the villagers Father?" I asked, "Yes I have Rosie" he replied, "we can communicate through the sailors who speak both languages. They say there is a large town about one day's ride by horse inland and a large city three days from their village. They trade with the town, providing sea food and farm produce. Apparently they used to live by the sea many centuries ago but as the water rose during the Warming they had to move inland. It seems they have chosen a simple life with the land and sea providing their daily needs, very much as our people have done. However, the town they travel to seems a bit more advanced, like the one we originally sailed from, as they have those bicycles and other remnants of the ancient times." "That sounds intriguing Father" I said wistfully, "Wouldn't it be so interesting to find out more about this town?" Father's face began to brighten as he realised my curiosity was just like his own. I could see in his eyes that an idea was forming and he was thinking it through. "Do I get the feeling that, like me, you would like to explore this country?" he said teasingly, "Oh yes Father, can we?" I answered and that was the beginning of the next great adventure.

As we waited eagerly on the beach the Captain sent a sailor up into the boat for our luggage and promised to deliver our beautiful rug and other cargo to a holding company back on our own land. He was as intrigued as we were about the possibilities of advanced culture so giving us some dates in the future when he would return to see if we were waiting to go home, he wished us a safe journey. The villagers led us back to their settlement and offered us a fine horse and carriage at a very reasonable price with a stock of travel food for the journey along with a rough map of where we would find the town. Waving us goodbye as we trotted off down the road were most of the people of the village and it seemed like no time at all that they had disappeared into the distance. Father and I spent the rest of the day chatting happily as we made our way through the countryside. We did pass one or two farms along the way with friendly waves from the folk as they went about the daily business. Stopping for a rest and a bite to eat by a stream was such a pleasure and it allowed the horse to graze peacefully nearby. We made good time that day as the land was fairly flat and the road in good condition so it was as the sun was setting that we arrived in the town. The villagers had told us of a good place to stay in a travellers Inn where they would understand our language, so we made for this first. Although we were very tired as we had been up very early when we were dumped on the beach, we decided to take a walk through the town centre after finishing a delicious dinner.

This town was very like the one where we boarded the ship for the first time. The people were very friendly, although we couldn't understand the language. There were quite a few oddly built bicycles, some with little carts attached to carry goods. Although the markets were closed for the day we found a few shops with goods for sale and trade displayed in their windows, so I told Father I would like to return in the morning to look inside. He thought that a very good idea so we wandered back to the Inn for the night.

I slept very well that night. After sleeping in rough weather aboard ship and the full day of travel behind me I must have gone into a very deep sleep indeed. In the morning I found that Father had already discovered the breakfast served in the dining room so I broached the subject of exploring. He knew me well enough and had already anticipated that I would like to be off on my own and had exchanged a couple of his 'trinkets' for some local money. I never knew how he did it but I discovered that Father always seemed to be able to produce local money as we travelled. I found out later that he carried a small bag within his voluminous coat that held rings and other jewellery he had brought from home. Currency had changed so many times over the centuries since the climate caused many traditional ways of life to collapse. In our country most people traded goods and services with one another and there had developed a way of valuing these commodities. However, Father had begun to collect jewellery and precious stones since before I was born in order to be able to trade with those outside our society. Because he didn't produce crops or have animals to trade he had become somewhat of a go-between or agent for those who did. We always had plenty of food delivered to our door and I cannot remember ever having to do without anything important. So, leaving Father chatting to the Innkeeper I set off armed with my little purse of local money, searching for new experiences.

The local Market had opened earlier in the morning and were selling all manner of food and goods. There were fruits I had never seen before and many types of colourful vegetables. As I was deciding on a new taste experience I noticed a shop with things for the kitchen and household hanging in the window. I wandered over for a closer look. There were shiny metal pots, cups made of glass and china, gadgets to do all sorts of tasks and on a shelf at the back of the window some very, very old things that seemed to be there just to look at – not for sale. My curiosity getting the better of me I entered the shop for a closer look. As I was craning my neck to see in the window a lady, about Father's age, came over smiling at me. She had a very kindly face and I gathered that she owned the shop. She spoke some words I didn't understand so I said so. "Ah," she said and began to 'speak' using her hands. I pointed to one particularly curious object and, nodding her head she took it from its place then beckoned for me to join her at the counter. The item was quite odd, it was a metal stick and at one end it had a pair of sharp looking blades sitting in a sort of protective case. At the other end, which was very heavy, there was what looked like a long, soft white rope with a lump on the end. This held two prongs. I must have looked quite confused so the woman took out a pencil and some paper and began to draw. She drew a bowl, some food in the bowl, then she drew the gadget standing up in the bowl. Now she picked the thing up and pretended to use it. I didn't understand until she went to a cupboard and brought out something that I was very familiar with, a whisk. So this was some kind of whisk. The woman then drew what seemed like a wall, drew the prongs as if they were going into holes in the wall and said one word - "ELECTRIC". Now I understood. I had learned about electricity. It was a type of invisible power. The ancients had huge factories where they burnt coal that was dug up from monstrous mines. The burning of coal made this electricity until the people of the Earth began to get very sick from the smoke. It took many years before the electricity was eventually produced only from the sun, wind and water but by this time the Earth had begun to fight back against the Warming. The rising of the sea and other catastrophes changed everything. My father had told me that he believed there were still places in the world where electricity was being used and he hoped one day to see it in action.

So there I was, holding something that ran on electricity many centuries ago and I even knew what it was used for. Using pictures and hand signs and a few words I had picked up I asked the woman if she had ever seen electricity used but she shook her head then drew what seemed like a big town with lots of tall buildings and pointed towards the rising sun. It was then that I realised what she was saying, the City we had been told about must have electricity. How very exciting. I had read children's stories from ancient times that told of Time Travel. Although this wonder had never been developed, - that I knew of - I felt as though Father and I were going slowly back in time. The further we travelled away from home the further back we seemed to be going. Very excited about my discovery I thanked the woman in her own language and set off to find Father. I knew he would be just as keen as me to see what was off in the direction of the morning sun.

Sure enough, next morning we loaded up the carriage and set off in a north easterly direction with a rough map given to Father by the Innkeeper. He had been to the City and was able to fill our heads up with all sorts of wonderful pictures of the things we would see. Buildings taller than we had ever seen before, horseless vehicles, rows and rows of houses. Oh this would be a great adventure. We chatted away until it was time to rest the horse and have some refreshments and it was a beautiful day to explore the land we were travelling through. To the north there were high mountains, covered in dense forest and capped with snow. The sun glinted off the snow and made it sparkle, I had seen snow from a distance before but not so much of it as was covering the tops of the mountains. We passed a few farm houses along the way and were greeted by friendly waves from the farmers. It felt good to be travelling, although I did miss my friends at the

Community. Travelling light was easy for me as I always wore simple clothes and I was used to not having many possessions. We were able to buy food along the way from the farms and little markets and the first night we found a farmhouse that had spare rooms they rented out to travellers complete with an evening meal and breakfast and food and shelter for our horse. The farmer had learned to speak the 'common tongue' of travellers, as had we by now, so he explained that there was a small village on the road where we could spend the next night in a Tavern. He said the villages would become more frequent as we neared the City. We settled in for the night with a feeling of satisfaction that we were well on our way.

I recalled much later in life the stories of the Climate Catastrophe and I spent many hours telling this to the children of our village. We knew that many cities had been deserted when the seas had risen and the air had become too polluted for people to breath. Food prices had risen so much because the cost of transporting it had become very expensive due to fuel shortage and so people had begun to leave the cities and move to country towns and communities. Here they could grow their own food. As the coal mines were forced to close down, electricity was very hard to maintain in the cities where small towns made their own from the sun and wind, the same thing happened to transport. Eventually the big cities began to close down altogether. It seems that once the coal and oil began to dry up it had a roll on effect with manufacturing and engineering. People began to recycle as much as they could and eventually many things disappeared that needed coal and oil to produce.

Because of my knowledge of the past I was very interested in what had survived from ancient times in this city and when we were on the last leg of our journey I found myself scanning the horizon for signs of large buildings. When they appeared suddenly in a valley beneath the high path we were travelling on Father stopped the horse and we climbed down to stare in amazement. There it was, buildings taller than we had ever seen before with shiny glass panels all over their roofs and windmills on every high spot. I could only stand there with my mouth open in amazement when Father took my hand and suggested we stop for a while, rest the horse and take in the view.

CHAPTER 12 – THE CITY OF THE SUN

There were many, many buildings of different shapes and sizes. We found out later that the shiny glass panels on the roofs produced electric power, as did the windmills. As we descended down the hill to the city there were many farms, big and small, growing rows and rows of vegetables and groves of fruit trees lined up across the fields. There were enclosures with ducks, geese and chickens running around and a huge lake that seemed to feed water through large pipes towards the city. It was hard to take it all in but we travelled slowly, vowing to come back and look over these amazing farms once we had looked around the city. As we got closer we noticed many different kinds of wheeled vehicles. Some were large with wagons on the back full of goods and others were just big enough for two people. They made no noise and seemed to move by magic as there were no horses pulling them along. We discovered these were powered by the sun and were 'fuelled' as they went along the road by some amazing energy that was fed up from the ground. I have since read some of the books I brought home with me about this solar energy and find it quite fascinating. Perhaps we will introduce it to our people one day – perhaps. One thing we did understand were the use of bicycles. There were many, many of these, some with three or four wheels but most with only two. There were quite a few with little wagons being pulled behind with children in them. Oh it was so much to take in.

Finding Bicycles

We eventually pulled up at what seemed like a Tavern and Father went inside to see if we could stay there. He came back a few minutes later to tell me we could stay and to take the horse and carriage around the back where there was a stable. Many travellers here used horses to carry them about. We were so tired from our day that we decided to rest for the night and explore the city the next day. My room was very comfortable and it had an amazing thing. The lady who took me to my room put her hand on the wall beside the door and pressed a button. I could not believe my eyes as the room lit up suddenly. She smiled and showed me how to switch it off again. I had experienced my first electric light!

As I sit now recalling the amazing things we saw in the next few days I have come to realise the incredible changes that had taken place over the centuries since what was called the "Climate Catastrophe". I have been taught to honour the Earth and all that she produces, this is taught to us all as children. *Look after the Earth and She will look after you*' is the basis of our upbringing. Whilst in the City I heard the tales of massive destruction by mines and industry and I understood why the Earth fought back. I was invited to visit a vast school they called a University where there was a room showing ancient pictures and objects no longer in use. There had once been enough oil taken from the Earth to make something called 'plastic' that was turned into many things. Plastic was now nearing its last recycling point so other materials have been invented to take its place. Bamboo, hemp, wood and other natural things were turned into much of the everyday useful items that were in use. There were unusual metals that had replaced steel, but the food that was eaten all came from the big farms we had seen and it all travelled in each day to the markets. The smell of newly baked bread each morning reminded me of home and the herbs that grew in the street gardens for people to help themselves reminded me of my life in the Community. Thinking of home I decided to stop in at a spiritual garden I had seen along the way. It was beautifully set out with shady trees, flower beds and many places to sit and contemplate. Taking a seat in the shade I placed my purchases down beside me and closed my eyes for a moment. After a while I felt the presence of someone and opened my eyes to find a tall elegant woman standing nearby. "I didn't want to disturb you" she said with a smile, but you look like you have travelled here from somewhere quite different. Can I ask you where you are from?" "Certainly" I replied, "I am travelling with my father and we have come a very long way. Why don't you sit beside me and I will tell you all about it." She sat down and we had a very long conversation about my travels. After a while she invited me to come along to where she shared a home with a group of women who sounded a bit like my own Community. However, they didn't have the space to grow food and herbs as we did so they did work in the communities around them and were paid in food. They had been doing this for centuries apparently and were known for their charity and healing work. I did enjoy spending some time there and I think it reminded me that I too had responsibilities within my village. I was just leaving when I heard raised voices. My host gently ushered me outside and explained. "We have one member of our community who has never settled in. Apparently she heard of your visit and wanted to ask you many questions about your home. We find this is very unacceptable as we try to treat everyone's personal life as sacred. Please, don't concern yourself. This member of our community is very restless and I don't want to spoil your visit." As she took me to the outer gate she gave me a hug and wished me a safe journey.

It wasn't long before I began to be homesick and so I approached Father one evening to see how he was feeling. "I understand how you feel" he said quietly, "this is all so incredible and very hard to take in. We shall spend a few more days here then make our way back. You realise that you will have to keep all this between you and I back home. Everything there is so simple the people would think we were telling tall stories. Lights that come on with a press of a button, vehicles that move very fast without horses, food that cooks without fire and keeps cold in a box, water, hot or cold, that is available in every building without a hand pump. So many unbelievable things. No, we can never discuss this unless we are by ourselves. Perhaps one day, if someone from the village is heading off to travel the world we could tell them, but not otherwise. Tomorrow we shall explore some more then start making plans to leave."

The next morning we left our rooms early to explore the city one more time. There was so much to see and I had decided to buy myself one or two things to take home, one of these things would be a book as they were very difficult to get hold of back home. Leaving Father to do his own exploring I walked through the shopping area until I found a book shop. Oh so many books to choose from that I had to decide to narrow my search down to something that would be useful. There were many about the great Climate Catastrophe and the ongoing trials of learning to live without earlier technology. I found one that told of the end of most cities and how people had to adapt or perish. It must have been so hard for the first twenty or so years as the only people who managed were those who had tried to change their ways before it all collapsed and those who had technical knowledge to make things work. The second book I bought was a Dictionary of the common tongue, a book of words and their meanings. That would be handy for teaching myself and others to understand the world outside our quiet and peaceful country. Armed with my purchases I found a place with free information on living without technology and rummaged through to find what could be a benefit back home. There were some interesting writings on growing food and looking after animals that would be handy and I was given a map of the city.

I met up with Father for lunch and he suggested that we visit what was referred to as the 'old city' where the ancient people had lived. The archaeologists and historians had been hard at work, carefully working their way through the ruins of long abandoned buildings. So far they had dated the buildings and artefacts from 2080 back many centuries to a time when there had been very similar lifestyle to the land where Father and I lived. We found a place where artefacts were being stored and asked permission to look around. I was given a book to take around with us that would explain what the items were, so we set off to explore. "Look at this Father" I exclaimed as we came to a stack of items with some attached to one another.

"The book calls them 'computers' and says they were storage devices to keep information in. It says that they were in every home and workplace. Oh Father, imagine having something like that, full of all sorts of information. It says they took the place of books for a very long time but that when the huge power generators closed down no one could use them any-more. At least we still have our books. And this looks interesting, it says you used it to play music. I saw something like it where we are staying, you press a button and music plays. The lady who showed me explained that you put it in the sun during the day for a while and you can listen to music at night." There was so much to see and as we wandered amongst the artefacts I became quite pensive. I was thinking of how different our lives were and whether or not I would like to live this way with things that required so much energy to run. The information book suggested that it was this power usage that eventually caused the Climate Catastrophe that changed the world forever. At the end of our visit I returned the book to the person in charge and we made our way back through the City. It was late in the day and the streets were emptying of people and as the sun went down the lights were coming on in the buildings. It was time for dinner when we arrived and as it was our last night there Father suggested we go somewhere nice for our meal. Tomorrow we would collect our horse and carriage and leave all this behind.

Over dinner that night I asked Father, "Do you think we will ever have electricity and vehicles that are powered by the sun?" He smiled and answered, "Perhaps one day my sweet, I may not live to see it but you may. I don't know that I am in a hurry to see that day. After all, it was technology that caused its own downfall and it has taken a few hundred years for the Earth to settle down again." I squeezed his hand, "Maybe you are right. We are happy in our lives and we have all that knowledge of healing, our farmers know how to grow plenty of good food and there are no wars any more. Perhaps it's best to leave well enough alone. I think I will keep all this to myself for quite a while."

We finished our dinner and made our way back to our accommodation. Tomorrow we would be on our way. It seems we had met with a place commonly known as The City Of The Sun.

CHAPTER 13 - RETROSPECTION

On our slow journey back towards the coast and our rendezvous with the ship we spent many hours talking of the wonders we had seen. Father was concerned that I would no longer be content with my life back home. He talked of the possibility that I might want to return to this place of wonders in the future in order to learn more of their technology and I have to admit that my mind was full of questions that may never be answered. I had seen people my age with clothes that clung to their bodies, driving around in those sun powered cars. I had spoken to one or two who could speak the common tongue and they used words with meanings that I could not even fathom. No, I decided, it was not for me but I was so very glad to have seen it all. We enjoyed the journey back, each day was sunny and warm and eventually we saw the sea in the distance. What wonders this world has in its' bosom and as Father reminded me there was so much more to see. Would I ever be content again to live my quiet life back in the Community? I would just have to wait and see.

The ship was only a few days away when we arrived in the fishing community. The people welcomed us back as if we were old friends and questioned us for hours about our adventure. Father decided to spend some time out with the fishermen and I stayed to learn about the way these people cooked their food and lived their normal lives. After the excitement of the City it was very nice to relax with peaceful and simple people for a few days. However, when the ship was sighted off shore and we were taken out in a small boat to climb aboard I really was ready to go home.

Travelling on the seas was a delight to me. I felt the rise and fall of the ocean as if the very Earth herself was breathing in and out. In the early mornings I was left alone on a quiet part of the deck where I could meditate on my journey with Father and make decisions on how much of this new found information I could pass on in order to make life a little easier on the people at home. In conversation with one of the farmers delivering his produce to market in the City I discovered that they were using an ancient method called Permaculture. I had read of this once when I had one of Father's books on farming. So much of this method was already being used as normal practice, however this farmer had explained they had set up their gardens with Permaculture right from the start and it meant that they used very little water on their crops. We had discussed many things that morning and I did feel that there was no harm in passing this on. Another thing that I felt would do no harm was the possibility of building up stocks of our dried herbal preparations and carrying them to the harbour town once or twice a year to trade. I had discovered that although these medications were commonly used they were limited in their supply. And so it was that I used my idle time on the sea voyage to work out ways that I could use my store of new information. When our voyage came to an end I had a head full of ideas to take back home.

The ship arrived in the harbour with the early morning sun glinting off the sea. The seas had been very calm with just enough wind to keep the sails full and our speed to the satisfaction of the Captain. Once again I leaned on the rail watching the sailors throw the huge, heavy ropes ashore to be tied to the wharf. There was much excitement as our ship arrived as the Captain had been on a journey of trade and the hold was full of exotic items to be sold or traded in the shops and markets. A line of carts was waiting on the wharf and groups of men were being employed to unload the ship and load the carts. We waited on board until all the activity had quietened down so we could farewell our Captain, so I did enjoy watching the busy workers going about their tasks. A large crane was brought onto the ship and the bundles and boxes were lifted up into the air and deposited carefully over the side. Finally it was time for us to leave, so with our baggage in hand we said our farewells. The crew were all waiting to say goodbye as well so it was with a bit of a tear in my eye that I shook hands with every one of them. The cook gave me a hug as I went by and pressed a parcel into my hands. "To help you on your journey home" he said. Later I found that it was full of the delicious biscuits he would produce every morning from his little oven.

Finding Bicycles

Finally away from the ship Father and I made our way to the same Inn we had stayed in when we arrived the first time and were pleased to find that the Captain had told them we might be coming. After leaving our luggage behind we went off to find our horse and cart and I do believe the horse was pleased to see us. The carpets and other items that we had bought on the outward journey had been stowed in a warehouse so Father went off to arrange for them to be delivered home while I went for a walk around the town one last time. I bought some sewing items for the Community and some bright coloured wool that would make wonderful warm socks for next winter. It was well into the day when I met up with Father in a tea room and we discussed our trip home the next day. So it was with a happy heart that we returned to the Inn for a good night's sleep ready for an early start.

I do believe the horse knew he was heading home as his head was held high and he stepped very lively indeed as we went on our way. Bye the time we reached Father's house the cook's biscuits were all gone and we were both ready for a bath and an early night.

Finding Bicycles

Those few days on the road had finished the adventure off very well indeed.

I did finally get back home to the Community and everyone was clamouring to hear of my adventures. However, I kept the stories simple and did not talk about the technology I saw or the amazing thing called electricity. Time would tell if I would divulge this. We did begin to make up the herbal preparations and essential oils to trade but Father arranged for them to be taken into the harbour town to his agent there and over the time we received some very good items in trade. So it was a few years before I saw the town again. I was content.

CHAPTER 14 - RESPONSIBILITY

My return to the Community was so very peaceful at first that life just seemed to float along. During my absence a new herb garden had been planted out with plants donated from around the country by travellers. There were some amazing healing herbs that I had never heard of and it was with great pleasure that I found myself in a group learning of their properties and uses. We were marshalled into one of the out buildings where Pennyroyal had set up bunches of different herbs and flowers. "Please gather around" she called, "it is important that you can all see what I am doing. These are herbs that are new to us and now that they have grown to a stage where we can pick them it is time to learn their uses." She proceeded to select one of the bunches and began to explain. It was a very good morning and we all went away with so much new information in our heads. The younger girls were to head down into the garden to weed and tend the new plants while I and two others were taken off into the hut where the oils were distilled. I did enjoy this process of producing oils and simples and by the end of the day I had bottled up several different oils for our Community healing woman. I had always shown an interest in this so was taken under wing to do a six month session of learning. Before long all the memories of my journey went to the back of my mind as I once more settled into the routine of the Community. Peace.

When I had been in the Community for about ten years I was approached one morning by Violet who asked me to join her and our senior members in the forest glade where we held most of our rituals. Intrigued by this request I changed into my formal robes and followed them along the winding path to the clearing. There the ancient, gnarled old leafy trees formed a canopy that allowed some sunshine through but kept the area so very cool. We had no altars or other items within our beliefs so I was invited to sit on the grass in a circle with the others. A few moments were spent in quiet contemplation then Violet began to speak. "Rosalind, you have been with us for some time now and during this time you have learned many things. You have become a teacher, a healer and a mentor for the other young ones. I am now reaching an age where I would like to relinquish my responsibilities as leader and it is with a glad heart that I know there are others to take my place. Although you are too young to take on that senior role we would like to invite you to become one of those who advise the younger members in both their training and their lives. You would be able to carry out such duties that you now enjoy such as your garden work but you would no longer need to do your share of the more physical tasks that are required of the young. We do believe that you are ready for this extra responsibility and eventually, you never know, you may end up being leader of this Community when those of us in our elder years pass on. So, what do you think?" Well, I didn't expect this, I had been happy going along

doing whatever was expected of me but I knew an answer was required. "Of course I am very honoured to be given this opportunity," I replied, "I know that I will carry out these more responsible duties that is now required. One thing though, if my Father needs me to accompany him again will I be able to go?" Violet laughed and the others smiled as they remembered how excited I was when I returned from my travels. "Yes of course," she said, "we always encourage our members to spend time with family and travelling will only make you a more valued member of this Community. You brought back some very useful ideas when you came back. Cook is now producing different meals and the bright fabric that your Father sent us has made wonderful clothing for the village children. Your tale of the sea voyage has always been my favourite, even the shipwreck, so I shall enjoy any tales you bring back on future journeys. So, if this means you will accept this extra responsibility then we will begin your training by invoking a blessing on your future."
Everyone held hands, we closed our eyes and Pennyroyal asked the Earth, Air, Water and Fire energies

to bring empowerment to my training. We stayed for a while and finished with a small picnic that had been brought along. Along with my new responsibilities I was given a red plaited belt to wear over my robe as a sign of my 'promotion'. I was a very proud woman when we returned that day.

Over the next few weeks I attended Violet every morning. She would talk to me about the history of our community and show me things that had been made to commemorate many occasions over the years. Then one day she really surprised me when she produced a small box and handed it to me. Opening the box carefully I didn't know what to expect, certainly not what was in the box. It contained something I had seen in the City of the Sun, on the end of a chain was a timepiece called a fob watch. It was very ancient and had no similar likeness in our time. "It tells you what time of day it is" Violet explained, "you need to wind it up each day and although we like to tell the time by the sun this was the way people told the time centuries ago before the time of Technology. I have had this all my life and it was handed down through my family in this little box for several hundred years. Now I have no children to pass it on to I would like you to have it." Well, I was speechless. I had not told anyone about my visit to the City of The Sun and now I needed to tell Violet that I understood what this was in my hand. Choosing my words carefully I said. "Oh thank you so much Mother of my heart. I will cherish this for all my days. I do think though that it is time for me to tell you another story of my journey with Father. There was much more to it and Father and I had made a decision that our world was not ready for all that we saw. We saw wondrous sights on that journey, one of which was a city, a place of many tall buildings and mechanical things that were so amazing that I didn't take it all in. We spent some days there and I have to admit that if I was given an opportunity I would return and learn so much more. These people developed from those who left the huge cities on the coast hundreds of years ago and took much of the old technologies with them. When things like steel and plastic was no longer manufactured they made different kinds of materials to replace them. There was so much, but we did decide that it was best to keep quiet rather than make people wish they had more than what was possible here. When I spent time on the plains with Hetia she did hint that she knew some of what occurs over the oceans but had also decided to keep it to herself.

Oh Mother of my heart, did I do wrong keeping this from you?" Violet smiled and held my hand in hers. "You did right my love" she replied, "our beautiful, peaceful way of life should not be ruined by avarice and that is what would happen should most people find out about this other world. However, I should let you know that I too have this knowledge. When I was very young and still living at home we had a visitor from over the seas. My father was, like your father, a trader of sorts and he also had much knowledge of mechanical things. He would have been called an Engineer in the old days and our house was full of amazing inventions and gadgets that he either made or had found in his travels. This is where the watch came from. I do believe that you and I will have some wonderful conversations together but we will keep this to ourselves for now. Perhaps there will come a time to divulge such news but not now. So please, pour us some more tea from that pot on the table and let us continue this conversation." Oh I was so pleased that I finally had someone to talk to about the amazing things I had seen. We would spend many hours chatting over tea until Violet finally passed from this life about five years later.

CHAPTER 15 - THE HEALING EARTH

Over time life in the Community became tranquil as the seasons slowly changed the landscape around us. We had gentle winter snow for the first time in centuries and this caused much celebration among the simple village folk. They had stories read to them as children explaining that when the time was right, in the cold of winter not felt for hundreds of years, a beautiful soft, while blanket would cover parts of our land. There were pictures of this phenomenon showing children building little men of snow and of trees and buildings topped with white. The changing of the Earth's climate meant that only the very north and far south of the world would retain any snow or ice. And now it had returned to our land. The Earth Mother was finally healing herself. There was a great feast the day after the first snow fell. Our Village Green was turned into a huge picnic ground and people came for many miles around to join in. Piles of delicious food appeared with the people and the children were put to task to try and recreate a snow man. There had been cold weather for a few generations and I recall Father saying once that he thought we would see snow before too long. And there it was. Overnight there had been clouds forming and everyone expected heavy rain, but our delight in the morning surpassed all other events of that time. I remember rising from bed and, as was my habit, going to open the window for a breath of air. There it was, all white and soft. A little bird was standing on a fence post singing its little heart out at the joy of it all. I grabbed my warm cloak and ran outside, forgetting my shoes of course, so I had to retreat and plunge my cold feet into the warm boots I had bought all those years ago when Father and I went on our first adventure. The snow was amazing. By this time the whole Community was outside, the young ones picking up handfuls of the beautiful white snow and throwing it at each other and the Elders were smiling as they watched the antics of the young.

After the initial joy had begun to wear off we gathered together to give thanks to the Earth. She was showing us that all was healing and that she was forgiving her human occupants for the damage they had done so very long ago. There was a lot of books and stories of the Warming and the ruin of civilisation as it was in the 21st Century. Such a pity it was the final straw that was named the Climate Calamity that was a catalyst for change. I am always grateful that I was born at a time after the climate had begun to normalise. It would never be the same of course, there were too many changes but we finally had four seasons again instead of wet and dry and our summer days were tolerable once more. Places like the Plains of Parlat where I had stayed with Hetia for six months had changed so very drastically though that it would be many years before their land was green and lush again. However, there we were with snow and we made the most of it. Mind you it all melted away in two days but it has come again each year since then and there is a little more each year.

CHAPTER 16 - FATHER'S NEWS

I had tried to get home to see Father on a regular basis since our adventure, 'regular' meaning once every year, and during this time I had seen him

become restless for more travel and more adventures
and as he got into his middle years it seemed to me that
there was something out there that he needed to go
and see. One day we were sitting having a meal on one
of my visits, it was a beautiful day and we were
contemplating our lives since our great adventure to the
land of the People of The Sun. During this conversation
Father dropped his little bombshell. "I have made a
decision Rosie, that rather than stay here for the rest of
my life and grow old in my chair I am going to go and
have a look at the world. I have been in touch with our
sea captain and he has told me that there is always a
cabin for me on board ship. If I would like to give them
a bit of a hand on the journey I could have my cabin for
free. He has just sent me a message to say that he will
be at the docks in a few weeks' time if I would like to be
there. So, I have decided that I am going to do that. I
have made arrangements here so that the property will
be managed and the business will be run properly in my
absence. There will be everything that you may require
while I am away, it will be supplied for you. This time
Rosie I will be away for some time so I do suggest that

perhaps I go and have a look at the world then take you

with me on another journey in the future." Well that

set me back, I didn't expect that from Father, I thought

that he would be settled into his business and trading

for the rest of his days and quite happy with that life. As

you can imagine we were quite excited at Father's

prospects and so we made sure that everything was as

it should be around the house and when I left to return

to the Community in a few days Father was doing his

final arrangements.

During the following year I received messages

from Father, letters passed to me by travellers that gave

me the impression that he was having a very good time.

He had found that the world had not totally gone

backwards after the Climate Catastrophe, that there was

quite a few places that had retained technology and

adapted it to suit our modern conditions. So of course,

when I got a letter ten months later that he was

returning I was quite excited to go and spend time with

him and find out all about his adventures. I took leave

of the Community and made arrangements to travel. At

this stage I was no longer a young girl and it was not a

problem at all to travel on my own. There had been no activity from the bandits for the past couple of years and folk had been safely travelling over the land. I had acquired, from a farmer a little carriage and horse that would take me on my journey, so off I went.

My visit coincided with the celebrations of mid-summer. Traditionally this was held on the longest day of the year, however, over the centuries it had developed into a week-long celebration of the harvest of summer fruits and vegetables and feasts were set up with entertainment and dancing. This was planned by the people of each district according to what they produced in their area. Many centuries ago there was also a religious holiday where people gave gifts to friends and relatives and families got together just as we do today. The gift giving had been faded out over time. I had read that people were so involved in outdoing each other for bigger and better gifts that it became an activity only for the rich. The poor had gone back to the very ancient ways of getting together for family feasts with music and dancing. I do believe that our way of celebrating mid-summer is much more enjoyable. Some of the summer fruits were delicious and I did enjoy a plate full of melons and berries covered with fresh cream. Oh yes, I do enjoy these to this day.

As I arrived at Father's home young Thomas met me. He was quite the young man by then and as he walked alongside my carriage we chatted about what had been happening since we saw each other last. He was now helping his father run the place and was learning the management so that he could take over from his father one day. We got along well, Thomas and I, so it wasn't long before he burst out with the news that Father was planning a journey once more. "Oh sorry Rosie," he gushed, "I wasn't supposed to say anything to you. But I am very excited because while your father is away my father will look after his business and that means I get to manage everything else. It is a big responsibility and I have to show that I can do it." "Well," I said, "I am sure you are quite capable or else you wouldn't be given this chance. Meanwhile, let's get to the house so I can find out where my father is off to next. I won't mention to him that you have said anything and will act surprised."

Finding Bicycles

As I arrived at the house Father came out to greet me and I could see he was suntanned and bright eyed and how healthy he looked. Obviously travel and sea air had done him the world of good. Taking my bag from the carriage Father called to Thomas to take the horse and carriage away. "Well, don't you look well Father," I commented, "It appears that sea travel is good for you. I want to hear all about your travels and the wonders that you have seen, but first I need a nice cup of tea." Father laughed at my priorities and called to the kitchen for refreshments. We went into his study and settled in side by side on the two big leather chairs that we had spent so many hours sitting in together over the years. I loved this room, it was full of books and interesting things and right in the middle of the room was the beautiful rug we had bought on our journey across the sea. My rug, with the ancient being in the centre, was hanging in my room at the Community where I could sit and take in the serenity of it when I was alone.

We spent several hours sitting talking. Father showed me some of the interesting bits and pieces he had carried home. He hadn't bought anything big this time as he only had the space of his little cabin on the ship, so it was with much pleasure that I investigated these things he had brought home with him. There were coins from faraway places, sea shells so beautiful that they had pride of place in this room and little statues and trinkets he had picked up in marketplaces. "Now Rosie" he began after his long story about the sea journey, "I have some more news for you. One of the places that I went to as ship's crew was in the opposite direction to where you and I went together. The land was very cold, far to the north of here, and was covered in snow while we were there so I didn't get to explore very far. However, it will be spring there in a couple of months and I wondered if you would be interested in another journey of discovery with me?" "Oh yes Father" I replied with a grin from ear to ear, "when do we leave." "Don't you want to hear more about where it is first?" said father, "No, I really don't mind where we go, but yes I would like to know more about it. Where is it? How long will it take us to get there? What language do they speak?" "Whoa" replied Father, "One question at a time. First of all it is about ten week's sailing north then east and we have to go up a deep inlet or fjord. There are many rivers coming down to the sea so there is one in particular where we will leave the ship and take to a smaller boat. As it is cold there, even in spring, you will need warm clothes and those lovely warm boots that you bought yourself. They speak the common tongue because they have so many travellers visiting, so we will be able to talk to them. But the interesting thing is that their technology didn't really fade out during the Climate Calamity because they were already using wind and water to create power. Because they are a bit isolated they also were able to keep a lot of their mechanical things going. I do believe that you will be fascinated by some of the things that are there and I have found an old book with some information on these people that you can read. We have to wait a month before we leave here so I will let you know in plenty of time for you to go home and let them know before coming back. Meanwhile, let's enjoy the mid-summer celebrations together and you can stay for a week or so before you need to head home." Well, was I ever so excited that I kept asking Father questions over the next week. Most of which he could not answer of course, but I could only imagine what I was going to see. The book he gave me to read had very few pictures so I had to imagine from the descriptions what they were talking about. They were a very ancient people. Their ancestors were sea travellers and explorers and as a result they had gathered many traditions and habits from all over the world. At some point in history the area may have been settled by Vikings, so named from their habit of going off to sea to gain land and treasure which was referred to as "going a Viking". Many tales had been told of their ventures but from what I read they were just looking for better land to farm and raise their children. I became quite engrossed in reading about these ancient people, so by the time a messenger came to bring me to Father in early Spring I felt quite knowledgeable on the people of the far north. Of course the book was written centuries ago, so as you can imagine my ideas were so far wrong that I was in for a very big and pleasant surprise when I finally met them.

Finding Bicycles

As I loaded my bag full of warm clothes and my special boots into the little cart I would travel in I turned to say goodbye to my community once again. The young girls I had been teaching came and threw their arms around me, hugging me and, with tears in their eyes, let me know they were afraid that they wouldn't see me again. The older ones stood back before saying their farewells and of course, with their knowledge of my past ventures, wished me well and said they would ask the Universe to look after me on my journey. I promised to see them in a few months' time and climbed aboard my cart. I didn't want to look back as I left because I did feel that this journey would be much further and longer than before and some of the older women were becoming quite frail. Would I see them again in this life? Only the Mother knew the answer to that question. I was a few years older than the last time I set off on adventure and this time I felt the pull of departure more than before. However, it was a lovely sunny day and I was on my way.

The journey to Father's house was always a pleasure for me. I had become known to the hostels along the way and a room was always held for me when Father's messenger told them he was coming to take me home. I suppose that I have done that journey so many times now that it feels much shorter as well.

Arriving at the front door I was greeted, as usual, by Thomas. He seemed to have grown into a man rather quickly and his big smile always gave me the feeling of having a little brother. Father had his bags packed and ready for departure the next day, so we spent the day planning and talking about what we would find.

CHAPTER 17 - SAILING

The journey to the coast this time was familiar, even though I had only been that way once in each direction. We spent the time talking about all the possibilities that could occur and what we hoped to find. I told Father that I had read the book thoroughly and thought I would recognise the people. However he laughed and explained that the book was written a very long time ago and everything would have changed. Still, I was not disappointed because there would be so much to see and do anyway. I was well beyond the young girl that he took away last time and I suppose I was a lot more apprehensive as seems to happen as we grow older. Sometimes knowledge can hold us back from adventure and sometimes it is a good thing to prevent us from stumbling headlong into trouble. This time I had some idea of what to expect – so I thought.

Finding Bicycles

We arrived at the coast with a day to spare so we booked into the same place we stayed the time before and went for a walk around the town. This time I wasn't so surprised at the bicycles and other mechanical bits and pieces and told Father that I wouldn't mind taking one of these two wheeled wonders back with me on our return. He laughed at that but made no comment. There would be so many other wonders this time that he knew that I might forget all about the bicycles by the time we returned. We found a nice little cafe to have dinner and I decided to forgo my vegetarian regime for once and try some sea food. Father ordered a lobster between us and I have to admit that it was absolutely delicious. We stopped by to watch a play that was being held in the local community hall, it was very funny and by the time we wandered back to our accommodation I was ready for a good night's sleep. The last I would have on dry land for about ten weeks.

Our ship had tied up during the night, so by the time Father and I arrived at the wharf most of the cargo had been unloaded and new supplies were aboard but the hustle and bustle remained with so much to yet be done by the crew and shore men. The Captain met us

at the bottom of the gangway with a big smile on his

rugged, tanned face. He had grown a huge moustache

since I last saw him and I remarked on how handsome

he looked because it made him look quite cheeky. He

laughed at that and led us aboard. We had got on

wonderfully last time and he had treated me like family

to make sure my first sea journey was one to remember.

It certainly was! My baggage, small as it was, had been

stowed away in the same cabin I used last time and it

was with a pleasant familiarity that I entered the low

doorway and sat down on the bunk. The Captain had

taken the time to hang some pretty bits and pieces

around for my benefit and had included a jug and bowl

so I could wash myself in the privacy of my little space. I

smiled as I thought of our last journey together when he

nearly lost his ship in the storm. It had certainly turned

the journey into quite an adventure that I will never

forget. Seeing technology long forgotten in our land

being used and improved by those who had been able

to secure the knowledge from centuries past before the

Climate Catastrophe changed everything forever.

Finding Bicycles

Not wanting to miss our casting off I made my way up on deck. The crew were the same as before, apart from a couple of newcomers, so I was greeted with smiles and hellos as I walked around the familiar deck. I was just having a look over the side at the water when a siren sounded and we began to cast off. I felt my breath catch as the realisation that we were under way finally hit me. The ropes were untied from the dock and hauled aboard, the boat was pushed away by a couple of burly deck hands with long poles kept aboard for such purpose and when we had drifted away the first sails were unfurled. As the breeze picked up we began to slowly leave the wharf and made our way out to sea. Eventually all the sails were shaken out and we picked up speed. I knew the best place for me was out of the way so I found a place up near the wheel where there were fewer people who had very specific jobs to do and I watched the shore slowly disappearing into the distance. The sun was beginning to warm up and thankfully the sea was quite calm, as I once more accustomed myself to the movement of the ship. Father had, as was his way, changed into work clothes and was helping out. I discovered later that he had

made a deal with the Captain for the journey and he

was now part of the crew for this trip. He didn't need

the money, he did it because he had grown to love the

life. I thought that perhaps I could help out in the galley

this time, so when we could no longer see the shore I

made my way down to the galley to ask the cook if I

could help. He welcomed me with open arms, it was

the same cook as last time. "I would be delighted to

have your company and help" he said with a big smile.

"You can find an apron back there in the pantry then

come on over and I will show you where everything is

kept. We have a full crew this time but as before you

and your father are the only passengers. Or should I say

you are the only passenger because your father seems

to have joined the crew once more." We laughed over

this and I began my new 'job' as ship's cook's assistant. I

do enjoy cooking and even though there was a full crew

there was still less people than in our Community where

I often helped out in the kitchens. This time though I

did have to learn how to cook when the ship was rolling

from side to side – that was interesting. One of the joys

I discovered was fishing. I would sit for ages on a large box (brought out for the purpose) and with my fishing line dangling over the side of the ship managed to land quite a few very good size fish. This, of course, was the way fresh food was always available aboard because someone was always happy to spend their off duty time fishing. I made friends with a few large birds that would come and hover over me up on the lines in case I was careless with where I put my catch. However, I was given a large tub of water with a lid to keep my catch safe.

Since our last journey our Captain had returned to the city where they had all the solar energy and bought a wonderful set-up to bring lights onto the ship. There were two solar panels mounted above the bridge and a windmill to catch the wind at night when there was no sun, then there were wires that led down below to the kitchen and the common area called the Mess. The Captain explained to Father and I that he had decided to start adding such things to the ship to see how much difference it would make. The crew thought it a wonderful thing because at night they had better lights so see what they were doing, it also meant that on deck the old oil lanterns had been replaced with these wind powered lights which meant less danger from spillage and fire. I enjoyed it because I had brought along a couple of books to read so it meant that I could sit in the mess with the men in the evening and bury myself in a book. I do believe that this was the beginning of changes that were to come into my life that I could introduce slowly to my Community at home and make a difference to their lives. More about that later on.

We had been heading north for quite some time keeping the land in sight on our starboard side. By this method we were able to follow our journey on a map Father had brought along. The days were so relaxing that when Captain eventually announced that we were going ashore soon I was almost disappointed. The sea had been fairly calm and the days sunny – what more could I want. The ship had turned towards the East into a deep bay where we spent most of the day carefully making our way in towards the fjords. The huge mountains seem to go up forever and one of the crew explained that most of them went down into the ocean as deep as they were high. As it was spring the snow was melting and this resulted in beautiful waterfalls down the sides of these monoliths. I was fascinated as we went further away from the open sea and made our way around the headland that was on our starboard side. The Captain explained that it was originally called Canada and that it was one of the first countries, many centuries ago, to embrace the energy production that would eventually save most of the world from falling apart when the oil ran out and the coal production was banned throughout the whole planet. Now it had another name, quite hard to pronounce, in its original native tongue. Travelling south now we had to make our way between many islands until late in the evening we came to rest at a very busy town with a long jetty jutting out into the water.

We spent the night in this very busy little town where we loaded up with fresh food and water for the next leg of our journey. It was strange sleeping that night with only a gentle rocking and I was surprised to find that when I went ashore my legs wanted to walk as if I was still on the ship. It took a while to get my 'land legs' back as Father and I went off to explore and buy a meal in one of the local taverns. Nothing was too special about this town except that they had electric lights and other technology that we had experienced before so it was the first time since coming home from our last journey that I had the chance to be in a very well lit space. The lights on the ship were quite dim in comparison because it didn't have very large battery storage. This was different. We could walk down the street with electric lights showing our way and the tavern was very well lit with lots of light globes. The owner told Father that they had their own battery storage out the back and lots of panels on the roof but in winter they relied on wind power to keep the batteries charged up. Fascinating.

The next morning we set sail once again and this time we began to head north going deeper into the fjords and well away from the open sea. On our last stopover the cook had brought aboard some salted and smoked fish for us to try and although at first I found it a bit too salty my mouth started to get used to it. He explained that people had been drying, salting and smoking fish in this region for thousands of years to see them through their very cold winters when a lot of the water ices over and they can only catch fresh fish by cutting holes in the ice. Brrr, I didn't fancy that at all. By now we could see the land on both sides of the ship and eventually we came to the place where Father and I would leave the ship for a few months and board a smaller boat that would take us into the shallower waters far away from the sea. It was with a bit of sadness that we left the Captain and crew behind but with a promise that they would pick us up in a few months time they waved us goodbye on our new transport. This boat was crewed by three tall, fair headed fishermen who would normally be out fishing but had taken the opportunity to earn a bit of money ferrying us up into the countryside. There were many rivers to take us inland and Father explained to me that when the seas had risen many new rivers were formed. Some villages and towns were flooded and the people had moved further up inland away from the water, so we would have to eventually leave the boats altogether and walk or ride for a day to reach our destination. I was very excited at this and as I shouldered my old bag and made to leave the smaller boat I felt that surge of excitement once again. We negotiated with a local to hire his horse and wagon with the promise that we would leave it with his agent in the place we were heading. The track was quite well formed as it had been there for hundreds of years and there were even remnants of an old tarred surface from centuries ago that had been built for the motorised vehicles that used to frequent the land. The man did tell us that once we reached our destination we could hire a motorised vehicle that ran on electricity but they were very expensive. Hmm, that might be interesting. But Father explained that we didn't have enough of the local money but if we stayed for a couple of months we could buy two second hand bicycles. Now that did get me interested.

CHAPTER 18 - ARRIVING NORTH

The road we travelled headed north-east according to the sun. I had been learning how to find my way by the sun and at night by the stars and moon when I was aboard the ship. It's all to do with your shadow during the day and the position of certain star formations at night. It was a fascinating thing to learn and now I had the chance to put it into practice. We travelled for a whole day and by late afternoon we could see the buildings ahead of us. This was not as big a city as we had found on our first adventure but it was much bigger than the coastal town where we caught our ship from. As we neared the town there seemed to be many folk travelling outwards. Father explained that this was a town where people came in to work during the day but lived in their little farms at night where they grew much of their own food. This had been encouraged many, many years ago when it became expensive to cart huge loads of food into the town. By growing much of their own food these people were well fed and seemed to be quite healthy. As it was just into spring the days were still reasonably short but we arrived before it became too dark and found a tavern that the man who owned the horse had told us about. They had two really nice rooms available so we put our things away and went in search of dinner. It would be soon enough in the morning to take our horse to the Agent and, I thought excitedly, to find ourselves a bicycle each. Our food was a pleasant surprise, this town ate mostly vegetables and dairy products so as I was supposed to be as much a vegetarian as I could be it suited me right down to the ground. After dinner we settled down in the tavern's main room and began to "feel" our way into the language and ways of the locals. Most of the people were quite tall and very fair of hair and skin. As the sun didn't stay out much during the colder months and this was the beginning of Spring it was no wonder that they were quite pale. Father managed to get into a conversation with two local men and as I was sitting comfortably in front of a lovely fire I managed to nod off in no time. Next thing I knew Father was nudging me awake - "Come on sleepyhead" he said with a smile, "time you got into your bed". I have to admit that I wasn't long in bed before I was fast asleep.

The next day was sunny and warm as we left the tavern to explore the town. Father had made enquiries as to where we could find a more permanent dwelling as we were to stay for a couple of months. There was a place that rented out small cottages for short periods so we decided to find them first of all. Walking among the locals that morning we realised that most people were wearing short sleeved shirts where we were bundled up in our long sleeves and coats. I supposed that it wouldn't take too long to acclimatise but I hadn't really packed up too many warm weather clothes. Soon we found where the shops and businesses were and were directed to the people who rented the houses. Father spoke to someone who gave him keys to two places for us to look at so off we went. The first one was perched on the top of a hill overlooking the countryside and seemed to be ideal until we went indoors. There was little furniture and it was painted a horrid shade of green all through inside. I know I couldn't have been happy there so suggested we try the next one. Well, what a difference. As we stepped through the front door I was taken by surprise. Someone had taken a lot of trouble to make it feel very homely. There was a fireplace with two huge comfortable chairs in front, a sweet little kitchen with table and chairs and two nice cosy bedrooms. The bathroom was attached to the back with a composting toilet, something I had managed to get used to on our last journey, and there was a lovely big, deep bath. Oh yes, I could be comfortable living here for a couple of months. The market was just down the road where we could buy all our food and there were all sorts of interesting places to visit in the area. Once we had deposited our bags we dropped the horse and cart off at the Agent we had been instructed to deal with and when we mentioned that we were after a couple of bicycles he smiled and led us out the back. There was a row of various sized bicycles there and all were either for sale or rental. As I hadn't ridden one for some time now I was a bit shaky and Father was even more so but we chose a couple of stout ones and soon got the hang of them. Off we went. Father had decided to buy them outright because the man had said he would buy them back when we were ready to leave and we could get a horse and cart from him then too. Well, this was fun. I did enjoy the feeling of riding along. I had traded my long skirt for a pair of trousers that morning, of course I hoped we would get the bicycles, so it wasn't long before I was riding like a long term cyclist. There were many in the town, most people either walked or rode although there were vehicles for deliveries and those who were not able to get about very well. There were also little trailers on the back of some of the bicycles and little wagons for small children to ride in. I decided that I was definitely going to take a bicycle home this time but I would have to buy one in the town where we rejoined the larger ship or it might be difficult to get it in the small boat.

After we had exhausted our riding ability for the morning we stowed them away and planned our day. First of all I would need to buy food so off we went to the market. As we arrived I found a stall selling baskets so purchased a nice big one to carry the food I would buy. The stall owners told me that all the food in the town came from farms within one day's travel or from the sea where we had come ashore. Because of the long winters the people had always been able to store the fresh produce during the warmer weather for use when the snow covered the ground. One farmer ran his own stall and invited Father and I to visit his farm, which was just a couple of hours bicycle ride away, to see how they grew food all through the warmer and longer days. We decided that the next day would be good for this venture so made arrangements to see him there. He would have his son run the stall tomorrow and bade us farewell until then. Because this was the beginning of Spring there was only a small variety of fruit and vegetables available but we knew that before we left this town there would be much more. However, there was a great variety of preserved food such as pickles, jars of preserved apples and other fruit and there were plenty of fresh eggs. Further along the road we found a baker (just by using our noses actually) and with a lovely warm loaf tucked under Father's arm we made our way back to the cottage. We would have a lovely meal this night and looked forward to the longer evening where we could sit on the little back porch. This would become our favourite place to be in the evenings and with a little table we also began having our breakfast there each morning. By now the sun was up fairly early and stayed there until a little after what we were used to. By the time we left the town to go home the days and nights would seem to be the same length.

One thing we had noticed was that all the houses were made of timber. This was not unusual at home but there were many stone or mud-brick houses back there. In this town timber was used because it grew so well in the hills and mountains. They had learned, many centuries ago, how to grow the forests sustainably so there was never a shortage. We were invited to go along to a factory where they used up all the odds and ends of the timber to make a sort of manufactured wood. By gluing all the bits together then pushing it through a sort of press, planks would come out the other side. This method was developed so long ago that no one knew exactly when but it meant that nothing of the tree was wasted and it was very strong. They had developed glues that were also natural and made from the sap of the trees themselves. We also found that they grew hemp during the warm weather that was turned into all sorts of things such as cloth and paper. Some of the people had built huge hot houses and were growing this and many other things right throughout the cold weather as well. It seems that they were very self sufficient in this town.

Our first day had been very busy so that night I slept like a baby and only woke up when the sun peeped through my curtains. I had chosen the bedroom that looked a bit "girly" and Father had chosen the one with lots of wood panelling. It wasn't difficult to choose and it didn't take me long to make the room my own for the time we were there. As soon as breakfast was eaten and cleared away we looked over the instructions the farmer had given us and packing a small bag of food and a water bottle we headed off on our trusty bicycles in the direction we were to go. He was right, it took a couple of hours on a well made road and we came to his front gate. There was a beautiful painted picture of a cow over the gate so we turned into the driveway and made our way to the house. The farmer's wife greeted us like old lost friends and showed us where to stow our transport. It wasn't long before we found ourselves out in the fields being shown around by the farmer and his wife. There were rows and rows of green stuff growing all around and he showed us his greenhouse where he started all the plants off while it was too cold to plant them out. He explained that they would grow them to about quarter size then, when the sun warmed the ground, they would plant them out to finish them off. They also had an orchard out the back full of apple trees. The apples were still very small but he explained that these would be ready in Autumn when they would all be picked and stored. I had bought a few rather dry looking apples at the market and it had been explained to me that these had been stored in a cellar all through winter and just a few taken out each week for market.

Later that day we headed back towards town and after a while father pointed out a side road that seemed to head into a forest. We turned off the main road and went off to explore this new direction. As we entered the trees it became considerably cooler and darker. I wasn't quite sure about it but as I was with father I kept quiet. I think it brought back memories of that first journey when I was "kidnapped" by the bandits. However, I swallowed my fears and continued on into the forest. After a while father held up his hand and we stopped. It was very quiet. There was no bird song or animal noises and that was a bit strange. We continued on foot and I was just about to suggest we go back when father silently pointed to a building almost hidden in the trees. "Let's see what that is" he said, "it looks like a factory or something. Strange that it is stuck way out here in the forest." We made our way closer until we came to a high wire fence. There were signs attached to the fence telling people to Keep Out. As we followed the fence along there was a gate with a guard sitting reading his book who stood up as he saw us approach. "No-one can get in without an escort." he announced, "You'll have to get one from the office in town." Well, this certainly got our interest up. "What is this place for?" asked father. "If you don't know you have no business here." answered the guard sternly "Now go away." We looked at each other and smiled. "Alright" said father and beckoning to me he turned, got on his bicycle and we both rode away. "I saw the name on the side of the building" father explained "and I'm fascinated. It seems we have seen history. That building may have been owned by a huge company from the past who used to make all sorts of technology. I thought they had collapsed about 2 centuries ago but it seems I'm wrong. With a big grin on Father's face I knew it meant we were going to investigate. We took off back to the road with me in hot pursuit.

Finding Bicycles

When we arrived back in town Father said he
wanted to go to the library and check up on a couple of
things and suggested I would like to go shopping. Well, I
knew what he was up to, he wanted to find out about
that building we had discovered. "No Father" I said,
"I'm coming with you because it would be much better
if both of us were looking. Now, what am I going to look
for?" He smiled and replied that we would be looking
through history books to see when that company could
have been operational. "It looked like they were up to
something" he said, "or why would they have a security
guard at the gate. No, I don't think it is long abandoned,
I think they are doing something there and I am curious.
Aren't you?" Of course I was. So off we went to the
library. There were so many books there and for me it
was like heaven. I had been an avid reader since I was a
small child and this place was like a treasure chest. I
couldn't believe how many books had survived over the
many centuries and it wasn't long before I was sitting at
a reading table surrounded by books. "What are you
reading?" father said, suddenly appearing at my
shoulder with a pile of books for himself. "There is so

much to see," I replied eagerly, "look at this one on herbal medicine and I have found one on cooking that uses a thing called a microwave." Father laughed and took that one from me. "This is of no use to you now" he said, "the microwave ovens disappeared when the electricity became scarce and was only produced locally with wind, sun and water. People went back to cooking the old way with wood stoves or oil produced from the vegetation. However, the one on herbal medicine should be useful. You can borrow the book from the library for a while so why not take that back with you to read in the evenings. At the moment though I'd like your help. These are old news items put together in book form so people can go through them. They are in date order so if we start about the time of the Climate Catastrophe and work our way to now we might find out something." I realised this was going to be quite a momentous task, but Father being who he was would not give up until he found something. So we began. It was about 2 hours later when the lady came over and told us she was closing up for the night and we had not found anything about the factory in the woods. So I did what we should have done in the first place. "Do you know anything about the factory in the woods that looks like it belonged to a technology company?" I asked. Not really expecting an answer. "Oh yes" she replied with a smile, "they are doing some experiments up there to see if they can get some old technology working. If you want to have a look inside I can ask my brother, he works for them."

I think I may have been quite stunned by that answer but Father certainly looked sheepish. After making arrangements to meet with her brother we headed for home. "I suppose I should have asked her in the first place." Father admitted "I thought it must be quite the secret the way they had a guard on the gate, but it looks like they are just keeping it safe from vandals and the like. I am quite excited though, this is quite an opportunity to see what there is left of the old technology."

With the book on herbs tucked under my arm we headed back to our cottage looking forward to the next day of exploration.

Finding Bicycles

CHAPTER 19 – WONDERFUL SIGHTS

We had an early breakfast that next morning and with a small bundle of food for the day we mounted our trusty bicycles and headed off to meet up with the librarian's brother at the factory. It was quite a cool day so we made good time and it wasn't long before we arrived at the gate to be met by the security guard. This time however he smiled and opened the gate for us. "Come with me" he said, "you are to meet Professor Stuart inside." He led us down between two of the buildings and through a rather impressive but empty office space. "This used to be full of staff many years ago" he explained, "but that was about 300 years ago. The historians have cleaned it up and tried to make it like it would have been. There were some old pictures in the library from those days so they had something to copy. Anyway, these days we are only using the main factory area inside." We followed him through a series of doors and hallways until we came to a brightly lit area where several people were working. We had seen machines from the collapse of technology but this time there seemed to be some that were actually working.

Finding Bicycles

Father was fascinated and once we had met the Professor he seemed to forget I was with him and went off to investigate. Leaving me to my own devices was not a bad thing though. I was also fascinated and began to do some poking about for myself. I was about to push a button to see what would happen when a young woman appeared at my elbow. "I wouldn't do that if I were you." she said quietly, "You were about to turn on a computer that the Professor has been working on and I don't think he would like someone else doing that." "Oh I am sorry" I blustered, "it's just that I have been reading about this sort of thing and would love to see how they work." "Well, we won't play with that one," she replied "but if you come with me I will show you something a bit easier." I followed her into another room and there before me was an array of bits and pieces. "I am about to start one of these up." the woman said, "I have been charging the battery from the sun over the past 2 days and I think it will now work. The only trouble is that I have no idea what may be in it. There may be nothing at all because it has been dormant for a very long time. However, we have found these things they call memory sticks from the 21st century and they might actually have something on them. Shall we see what happens?" "Oh this is so exciting" I replied and I know I must have sounded like a little girl but I couldn't help myself.   She put the battery in the back and opened it up. There was a moment of intrigue as she pushed a button and waited. Little lights came on and after a while the glass she called a 'screen' lit up. We waited. Nothing. "Wait a bit longer" the woman suggested and fiddled with a few of the buttons. Next thing some words came up. "Oh" she said, "I will have to put some words and numbers in, I won't be a moment." She left the room for a while and came back with a book. "When the computers have been dormant for a long time" she explained, "you sometimes have to 'reboot' the system." As she put the words and numbers in I was fascinated that it began to show a whole list of words. After a while the screen cleared and there was a blue background with words and signs around it. "This is great" she said, "now I shall put this memory stick in the little slot and we'll see what's there." After a while she was able to find something and lo and behold there was a lot of pictures. "Wow" the woman exclaimed "this must have been someone's collection of pictures. Look at these."

We spent the next hour going through everything she could find until the computer began to flash a light. "Oh we are running out of battery" the woman explained. "We will have to shut it down and recharge it. But what a wonderful find. I am so happy you were able to share this with me." I thanked her and with a big smile across my face I left in search of Father. How wonderful this day was and it was with great sadness that we finally left it all behind. As we rode back to town Father turned to me and said "You know we have to keep this information to ourselves don't you? When we go back home this is way beyond what our people are capable of accepting and they are really not ready for such technology." I had to agree with him and there were many things I would have to keep to myself. Our time in this place was coming to an end soon and we would return to our quiet life on the other side of the world. Keeping this to myself would be hard but I knew it had to be done.

Finding Bicycles

It was by good chance the next morning that Father suggested we go for a walk around the city centre because there in the main street was an amazing sight (to me). Parked alongside the footpath was one of the electric vehicles that we had read about and seen occasionally out of the city on the roads. The City of the Sun had also been able to produce such vehicles. Father was very excited, as was I, so we ventured over to have a closer look. The "cabin" of the vehicle had four seats, two in the front and two in the back, and there was a panel of gadgets with what I knew was a steering wheel – like a small version of the one on the ship. While we were nosing about a man came up smiling and began talking to Father. I politely kept back a bit but was straining my ears to hear what was being said. Father turned, "This is the owner of the vehicle Rosie and he asked if we would like to go for a drive. What do you say". The grin on his face told me how he felt about it and of course I was very keen. So in we got. Now, I am quite adventurous and have been known to get up quite a speed on my bicycle but nothing prepared me for this. Although we left the edge of the road slowly it wasn't long before we were moving along at quite a pace. It was so quiet though that I thought we must have been floating. With the windows open there was quite a breeze coming in and my hair was flying out behind me and I am sure I must have looked like a child with a new toy because my cheeks were quite tight from grinning. It was amazing. We travelled around for about half an hour before he brought us back to where we started. When we got out Father asked to have a look at the engine and it was quite a while before he finally thanked the man and turned back to me. "Wouldn't it be great to have such a vehicle at home?" he said excitedly. "Yes Father, it would" I replied, "however we would need to have quite a lot of money to be able to bring one home and how on earth would we get it on the boat?" He realised I was kidding him and laughing we turned and made our way through the City. There would be many other wonderful things we would find that made this journey fascinating but the ride in the electric vehicle would be the best.

Having just a few days left I thought it would be

good to find out more about the technology that had disappeared from our land. The distance between continents had meant that many cultures such as ours had never recovered the ability to produce electricity or manufacture anything on a large scale. I was to find out that making electric vehicles needed electricity itself and much equipment and base materials that had not been seen on our continent for a few hundred years. Ours was a simple place where we were able to live in a simple manner and there was peace throughout the land. I had read about the wars and violence in the 20th and 21st centuries and much of it was caused by financial greed. Our home did not have this problem any more and we were all glad of that. Our money was basically reusing coins that had been around for centuries but mostly we traded goods and services. So to me, this land we were visiting was to learn what to avoid as much as what was still out there in the rest of the world.

I returned to the library where I had received so much help before and asked if there was anywhere where I could learn the more recent history of this place. I was given the address of the museum and off I went to find out more. I was met by a very helpful woman who knew almost all that could be learned about their history and she led me into the museum to show me around. One of the things she talked about was the way they made power for the electricity they used. One room was given over to this subject. When the Climate Catastrophe hit in earnest much of the power supply disappeared apart from the towns and cities where they had already turned away from coal and gas. Many buildings had solar panels or wind turbines and produced their own power. Even houses in those places produced their own. However, the support systems for this eventually disappeared. Factories that made these systems had to think of new ways to maintain their equipment. Some didn't bother, and those places just fell back to the time before electricity, as did our land. I was shown pictures, taken with what was called a camera, of the beginning of the end of technology as we knew it and I decided it was probably for the best that we stayed away from that way of life. Now the camera was of great interest to me as I had seen them about. The lady took me to another room where there were cameras from over a period of 200 years. She explained that after technology disappeared people had gone back to using the simple versions from the very early days and they were able to still take pictures. The hardest part was getting the film and developing it but there were people who still had that knowledge and so it all began once again as it had way back in the 1800s. She told me where I could buy such a camera and so it was there I headed off to when I left the museum.

The camera shop was fascinating. There were these huge wooden boxes and very small metal ones and they also had the film that you needed to take pictures. The man came over and we began to talk. He showed me how they worked and explained how you had to turn the film into pictures. He gave me a small booklet to read and left me to play with one that was set up as a demonstration. I found out how easy it was and asked the man to take my picture. He did so and asked me to come back in a few hours and he would have it developed. How exciting. So off I went to buy some lunch and came back later in the day. There I was, me, as clear as day. Just like I looked in a mirror. He gave me the photo and I asked how much the camera would cost. Well that was the end of that. It might have been old but it was very expensive. However, I was so happy with my photo that I went off back to our house grinning from ear to ear. When Father arrived later on I presented him with the photo. He was so proud I thought he would burst.

CHAPTER 20 – GOING HOME

As we finally arrived back at the boat that would take us home I looked around over my shoulder to the place where we had learned so much about the technology of the past. Could it be that the whole world was so far advanced to our present state and then revert back to what was described in the history books of the library as the "Middle Ages". Admittedly our country was very far from other continents and it seems that we had reverted further back than many other countries Father and I had visited. The lack of communication between continents meant that each area was advancing at it's own pace. Travel was reduced to sailing boats at sea and horse and carts on land which meant most folk didn't bother leaving their own area. A fact born out around our own country where most folk who lived in the country never travelled to a town or city.

The journey home was a peaceful one. The seas were calm and the weather fine and I spent many hours sitting quietly on deck contemplating the information I had gathered. I had books to read and it was during this journey that I began my journal, recording the memories of our adventures. I would have to keep this to myself of course, but the good thing about living in the Community of women was that of privacy. No one would ever intrude into my private space uninvited. The journal became my daily life on the boat, apart from spending time in the kitchen helping the cook. That was a pleasure I would not give up. Eventually we disembarked at the village by the sea and made our way to the inn. Our horse and cart were still there so we prepared to leave for home the next day. Meanwhile I took Father for a walk to the bicycle shop where I bought 2 bicycles to take home. One for me and one for anyone who would like to come riding with me. This was one enjoyment I would not leave behind. Throwing the 2 machines up on the cart the next morning we headed for home. Eventually, tired and happy I flung myself onto my old bed at Father's house and slept like a log.

When I arrived back in the Community with the 2 bicycles there was much excitement. I had no sooner offloaded them from my little cart than the youngest of our members took possession of the smaller one and, hitching up her skirts, climbed aboard. "I have seen one of these in a picture book when I was a child." she said with a great big smile. "I know you push the pedals with your feet and it should move. Can I please give it a go?" I picked up the other one and climbed on board. Showing everyone how to ride was so much fun and soon most of them had tried it out with much laughter and some small accidents. Eventually the bicycles were stowed away in a shed and we all went inside to prepare for the evening meal. It was so good to be home.

PROLOGUE

Fifteen years of peaceful life and the travels with Father along the way gave me a belief that I had chosen well to stay in this community of women. We all had our tasks and there was a harmony among us that gave rise to a certain complacency that this would last forever. However, our lives were to change as our newest member arrived one Spring morning.   We had lost poor old Violet during the last year, thankfully she passed peacefully in her sleep. We celebrated her life with a beautiful ritual in her favourite part of the garden and after her cremation we scattered her ashes amongst her flower beds.

I was in the herb garden when I heard the voices at the garden gate. Marigold was talking quite loudly, as she did. We thought she was getting deaf. However, this time she seemed to be having a discussion with the driver of the cart that brought our supplies from the Village. Leaving my gardening for a moment I walked around the corner to find a rather large woman with her back to me, dressed in robes I had seen during my travels in another country. I recalled that she must be a member of a spiritual order from the city with all the wind and solar energy. Living within a city they were more involved in the spiritual welfare of the inhabitants whereas we also looked after their health and the health of the land. Curiosity getting the better of me I wiped my soiled hands on the grass at my feet and walked up to the woman and Marigold. "Hello, I'm Rose" I introduced myself using the name given to me in the community. "I recognise your robes as being from a community I visited several years ago."

"Ah yes" she replied, "I was away when you came but I was told how you were part of this community and as I rather like the idea of living away from the cities I thought I would come and visit. I hope you don't mind. I probably should have sent a message ahead." With this she turned rather abruptly and walked towards our main building. I looked at Marigold and she at me and we followed on. It was obvious that this woman was much older than most of us so we would give her the respect we would give any elder and showed her into the room that was once occupied by Violet. "Would you mind waiting here please?" I asked, "I will gather our community together and let them know what is happening. We don't have a hierarchy here, all decisions are made around the table in the evening so if you would like to rest for a while I shall talk to the others about having a visitor or new community member." She looked quite taken aback at this but put her things on the bed and sat down in Violet's favourite soft chair.

Finding Bicycles

Gathering the others together in a quiet corner of the garden we began to discuss the new arrival. "I'm not sure about this." said Marigold, "She could have let us know by messenger that she was coming. Besides, she does seem a bit aloof. However, I am willing to give her the benefit of the doubt at least for a few weeks to see how she settles in." "Her community has very different ways to ours." I offered. "They spend a lot of time in prayer and meditation and when I was there I didn't see much in the way of a garden so I think we will need to ask her what she intends to do within our community." The others nodded their heads in agreement. In the end we decided to tell her she could stay for a while to see how she fitted in. I was given the task of letting her know so off I went.

"Can I come in?" I asked from the open door. "Yes of course" the newcomer replied. I entered and said "We have discussed your sudden arrival and have come to the decision that we would love you to stay for a while. Eventually you may like to stay on permanently but our lifestyle is very different from the one you lived before and you may not be happy here. So for now, if you wish, you can take over this room, it belonged to our dear Elder Violet who passed over some months ago. Please, settle in and meet us at our midday meal. We have no formality here so please feel free to wander around. I will see you in the dining area." As I went to leave our guest rose from the chair and came towards me. "None of you have asked me my name or why I have left my community so far away. Although I am grateful for that I do wish to let you know that I would like to stay here permanently. I have brought some ideas with me that we were using in my former community and I am hoping that you will encompass them. My name is Amala. It is an old name in my family but I understand your community takes on the name of flowers. This is lovely but very quaint and I don't believe that I will be doing it." With that comment she turned, sat back down in her chair and closed her eyes. I felt dismissed like a child, and this did not feel comfortable at all so I returned to the garden and the work I had been doing feeling like I had been admonished. I would have to speak to the others about that as it was not our way.

Finding Bicycles

When we sat down for our midday meal Amala had not yet arrived so I quickly told the others about her comment over names. "I know it shouldn't matter" I said, "but perhaps she will change her mind. Meanwhile I believe we should treat her as a guest and wait and see." As I was about to begin to eat Amala entered the room. Sitting at the end of the large table with the rest of us she assumed an air of superiority. This would not go down well so I silently went on with my meal and waited to see what would happen. All of a sudden Amala spoke. "You seem to be so backward here so I thought I would tell you about some improvements you could make. First of all your bathing and toilet facilities are so primitive. Having to wash in cold water and go to the toilet over what seems to be a pit in the ground is disgusting. I would like to organise someone from the village to come out and put in some running water and a proper toilet. I intend to stay here for some months and I need to feel comfortable. Also, there seems to be no kind of electric power, you will need to look into this for me. For now though I will eat my meal in silence." Well, we all looked at each other and almost choked on our food. Who did this woman think she was coming in and trying to change our world. I had seen the piped water and flushing toilets on my travels and although I knew what electric power was none of the others, in fact not many across our land, would have any idea what she was talking about. I decided that once Amala had left the room I would explain to the others what she had said to me and what I had seen in her country. In the meantime we all ate silently – which was unusual for our community.

"I would like to tell you what Amala was talking about." I explained to the group once Amala had left the dining room. "If you remember some time ago I told you about the amazing sights I had seen while travelling with my father. Well, one of the places we went to was where Amala's community live. You all know some of the history of the world before the Great Climate Catastrophe. Some countries were able to retain small amounts of the technology of the past and improve on them to suit the present. One of the results of this technology is called electricity. I think some of you know what I am talking about. Anyway, this particular city, and quite a few others as well, have developed this electricity using the wind and sun and some are using the power of running water. I won't explain the technical details but it means that we can produce some power to run lights instead of using oil or other fuel. In some cities they have enough of these windmills and sun batteries to have electric lights in every home or business. I know this sounds impossible but it is true. My father has some books written hundreds of years ago when people stopped burning coal to make power and used wind, sun and water. The other thing Amala was talking about was water that is piped into our buildings so we can just turn on a tap instead of carting water from the well. This is not difficult to do and I guess we could think about getting one of the farmers to come and put that in place. Some of the farms are already using piped water as they have done for hundreds of years. When she mentioned the fact that our toilets seem to be primitive to her she doesn't realise that it is much better for the land to have it the way we do. So we should not take any notice of her criticism in that area. So, any questions?"

Finding Bicycles

It took moments for what I had told them to sink in and then they seemed to all talk at once. The conversation went well through the afternoon and I was quite exhausted by the time we realised that the day was coming to an end and there was work to do. We had come to the decision to tell Amala that if she was staying with us she would not be able to make all the changes she talked about but that we would look into getting the running water because we all agreed that would be good. However, as the idea of electricity was beyond how we wanted to live she would have to put up with our candles and lamps. I offered to go and talk to her so I took a deep breath and knocked on her door.

It all went quite well I thought. Amala agreed that we could not do all the things she had suggested and that running water would be nice. However, I don't think she was too enamoured with the idea of our composting toilets. Oh well.

The following day I set off to go and visit one of the farmers just out of town. It was a beautiful day and I did enjoy walking about our countryside. The farmer was in his field when I approached so I climbed the fence and went to talk with him. He was delighted that we in the women's community were going to embrace the idea of running water and said he would work out what it would cost and let us know. Then of course he invited me in for a cup of tea and some of his wife's cake! The next thing I wanted to do was try and get hold of some of Father's books on how people lived their lives before the Catastrophe that would show the Community what electricity was all about so I hired a local man to ride to Father with a letter from me explaining what I needed and why. I was pleasantly surprised some days later when Father's cart pulled up outside and in he came with a box full of books. "Couldn't resist the personal touch" he said smiling, "I thought you might need some help explaining things. And I really could do with a nice cup of tea!" Laughing at this I led him into the kitchen and put the kettle on. It was lovely to have Father with me as it had been a little while.

That was the last time we spent any length of time together. A few months later Father set off on another one of his adventures as part of the crew of a different ship. He wrote to me from the docks as he was about to leave and said he would try to let me know where he was along the journey. I never heard from him again and discovered that he had left the ship in a place where he could travel overland to a civilisation that had retained all the technology of a time before the Climate Catastrophe. As most of the settlements were far inland they had continued on making their technology fit the climate. The only thing was communication and travel to other parts of the world. This had obviously meant they were cut off from the rest of humanity. However, upon reflection, it may have been where the Captain and his soldiers had come from that had allowed Hetia to rid her lands of the Horde of Doom. Who would know. It seemed that there was no-one who was interested enough to explore that idea and by then I could not leave the community. I wrote a letter to Hetia asking if this was possible but never received a reply. Upon reflection it may be that she didn't want to share that information or she could have passed on to her next life by then. It would always remain a mystery to me. As was my father's disappearance. At least he went off on an adventure. That was some consolation to me. But I did miss him. I received a letter from Father's solicitor telling me that I now owned Father's property as he had set this in motion before setting off on his adventure. I did leave the Community and went home to all the books and amazing souvenirs where I spent my years with the family I had grown up with. I had peace at last.

THE GREAT CLIMATE CATASTROPHE

It came to pass that The Earth could no longer tolerate what people had done to her, so She just wound up the heat. Over a year or two this melted the small amount of ice left on the north and south poles and the seas rose up to swallow huge cities and towns along the coastlines over a fairly short period of time. Some small islands over the planet disappeared under water never to be seen again. People on the larger islands and continents fled inland and tried to take over the smaller towns, but of course without power and water many of these city folk just didn't survive. Unlike the country folk who had been doing so for some time.

It took almost two hundred years once the sea stopped rising for everything to settle into a new normal. What was left was a dry, arid land with very few rivers and streams. Away from the coast where forests had stood since ancient times became a huge dry and dusty plain with scrubby bushes here and there. Some people knew that this was how the centre of the island had been for thousands of years but it was as though the whole country was drying up. Up in the hills and close to the coast it was still green where the air was a little cooler. The trees had created enough shade to keep the soil moist and if it did rain at all that's where it would fall. Some people moved into the hills though, but some of them were worried about forest fires because there had been plenty of those when the temperature rose.

Before the Climate Catastrophe the temperature began to be unbearable. First of all it just meant staying indoors or in shade during the middle of the day but then when the electric power was no longer available there was no cooling and heating in the buildings so many people in the cities just died. Old people, little babies and invalids just began to die from the heat or cold. It was far too hot for anyone but the healthy folk and older children who could always find some way to cool down and eventually the people who had survived began to adapt to the hotter weather.

THE OUTSIDE WORLD

Over the centuries since the great Climate Catastrophe, with communications and travel being so limited, our country gradually lost contact with most of the outside world. Although there was travel to the coastal towns, and some took this journey for business, the people had become used to their simple ways and left well enough alone. However, much of the outside world had not reverted to medieval times and had found new ways to rebuild their infrastructure and way of life. Because there was no longer air travel and the only ships that sailed the seas relied on wind power, countries in the southern hemisphere were once more isolated from the rest of world. However, there were cities and towns in other lands and their technology had adapted to what was still available.

RELIGION

Religion began to disappear when people came to realise that no God they had been praying to was making any difference to their lifestyles or the rising temperature, so they had begun to pray to the Earth Mother to help them grow crops and for the weather to be more reasonable. It was much easier to be able to just go outside and ask the Earth to let the seeds germinate than it was to go along to a church building and spend time on your knees. Oh yes, the Old Religion raised its' gentle head once again and people began to believe. The wind, rain and the sun could also be spoken to and asked for mercy. That was much more simple for these farmers and tradespeople. And so a new Old Religion grew from just a few believers to be the religion of choice for the whole country. Spirit Leaders and Shamans began to emerge once again and it seemed that was so much better for the beliefs of the people because with the cooling of the Earth many thought their prayers to the Spirits of Earth, Water and Sky had been answered.

Finding Bicycles

ABOUT THE AUTHOR

Living in a quiet Eco Village in Central Queensland, Australia has given Heather the time and energy to follow up on ideas that have been in the melting pot for many years. As a Freelance Journalist there was the satisfaction of letting readers know what was happening, however her storytelling gift was finally realised with the release of Under Her Protection in 2020. As a grandmother she has taken mental notes of how young people feel about Global Warming and how it will affect them later in life. Using this knowledge she has been able to put those ideas into her new release. The idea of a future on the Earth so different from the present following global warming gave a life to Hetia and her people and now Rosalind will explore how that future has played out.

BY THE SAME AUTHOR

UNDER HER PROTECTION - Paper back and Ebook
In a future following the Climate Catastrophe that changed the Earth forever, a gang of marauders are terrorising the people on the Plains of Parlat. Nothing has been able to stop them until a local Wise Woman, Hetia, decides enough is enough and with the help of others sets about to be rid of them once and for all. Good natural magic and a bit of help from a surprising source finally solves the problem

Finding Bicycles

Finding Bicycles